# THE TRAFALGAR ROSE

Beautiful auburn-haired Celeste awoke in a bordello to the realization that her memory had vanished. She had no idea why she had come to London; her past revealed only her name, the French she spoke, and a wild love for the sea. Her future, however, promised a haven on an English country estate, where she would discover undying passion for Lord Nelson's dashing lieutenant, Miles Stanley. But her new love could be doomed if her foggy memory revealed that she was French.

CLARE FRANCES HOLMES

THE
TRAFALGAR
ROSE

*Complete and Unabridged*

LINFORD
*Leicester*

First published in the
United States of America

First Linford Edition
published 1996

Copyright © 1981 by Clare Frances Holmes

British Library CIP Data

Holmes, Clare Frances
The Trafalgar rose.—Large print ed.—
Linford romance library
I. Title II. Series
823.914 [F]

ISBN 0-7089-7842-8

Published by
F. A. Thorpe (Publishing) Ltd.
Anstey, Leicestershire

Set by Words & Graphics Ltd.
Anstey, Leicestershire
Printed and bound in Great Britain by
T. J. Press (Padstow) Ltd., Padstow, Cornwall

This book is printed on acid-free paper

# Part One

Part One

# 1

I FELT the blow upon my head. I know that I sank to the ground. My face was pressed into the dank, malodorous flooring. I felt the pain spread from my head to my neck and shoulder. I cried out, but my voice was lost in the uproar. I tried to rise to my feet, but found that I could not move.

"You should not have hit her so hard, Robert," a rough, woman's voice was saying. "You struck her before. Once was enough. You do not know your own strength."

"Let me have her, Mrs. Magwich. I could teach the likes of her a thing or two." The voice was crude, callow; I guessed that the speaker was a young man. "She would soon learn the conditions of the game from me! She would early accept her situation

3

and her place in life."

"Don't talk such rubbish, Robert Lessing. You know young gentlemen of quality pay a high price to be the first with such as this capon. She is clearly untouched, and ready for it. Be off on the errand while I go to prepare her room."

"What is it you want?" the man's voice asked, and Mrs. Magwich replied, "the usual bottle of gin and a box of cheroots. Now make haste and get back quickly. It will be a busy night and I need you here."

I lay still, for indeed I could not move. That there was menace to me here, was clear. I was in less danger in this dark and unsavoury place, but what the danger was I could not, in my confused mind, comprehend.

I realized that the voices had stopped, and that I was temporarily alone. I managed to raise my head and to peer about me. I was obviously in the back premises of some establishment, but where this was, and what it represented I did not know.

Like a flash of revelation the thought came to me that I must escape. Somehow I must quit this house with its threat and base atmosphere. I looked at the filthy tables and chairs, the dripping water from the pump mouth, the stained and damp walls. There seemed to be nothing here to help me. Yet I knew that time was precious, that soon Mrs. Magwich and the man called Robert would return. I guessed that when that happened, there would be no escape from the purpose for which they had brought me here.

I managed to drag myself to my feet. The pain from my head and shoulders brought on a bout of nausea. Fighting the sensation down, I clung to the table, trying to gather together my scattered thoughts. I felt a faint breeze blow upon my face and turned my head toward this breath of fresh air. The thought came to me that Robert had left a back door open. That there was access from this shuttered room. I began to move towards a door which I saw now was ajar. I guessed that this would lead to a further passage, and so it proved to be.

I stood at the junction of two passages. One led into the darkness of a narrow corridor, the other towards what appeared to be the front of the house. I looked towards the brightness of the entrance foyer of this establishment. How different it was from the premises from which I was endeavouring to escape!

A chandelier shone, its brilliants winking as it moved in the air. I saw velvet chairs, brocade curtains, a French carpet. And Mrs. Magwich stood there talking to a young man.

I knew it was Mrs. Magwich, for I heard the young man repeat her name, as if she had been introducing herself. I saw that she was stout in build, strongly made. She was dressed in black silk with a bustle draped over her big hips and swelling abdomen. Her capacious bust was draped with a silk shawl and she wore a white cap upon her head.

Iron grey ringlets were arranged around her face. Her complexion was pale, her features rounded and rather squashed, as if she had suffered violence in her time. Though her clothes were expensive, they appeared stained and soiled. I now saw that the fittings of the front of her house were second-rate, misused and neglected. A smell of perfume, spirits and human perspiration wafted down the corridor.

I steadied myself against the lintel of the door. Truth to tell, I was obliged to rest for these few moments, before I could venture further. I looked at the young man who was listening to Mrs. Magwich, yet I observed him for less than a minute, since nausea again assailed me, and I was forced to close my eyes.

Yet in that brief time I saw that the young man was dressed in formal evening clothes with long tight trousers, and a cutaway coat. He wore a long black cloak, and when he moved I noted the flash of the crimson lining. I saw the silver knob of his stick glint in the light from the chandelier.

Then the front door opened, and another young man entered. He was of medium height, carelessly dressed with a wide, dough-coloured face. He was powerfully built and he rolled on his feet, as if in the pugilist's ring.

"Ah, Robert," said Mrs. Magwich. "Take the goods to the back, and attend to the package there. You will know where to take it, and Mimi will prepare her."

At these words, terror smote at me, and strength returned to my faltering limbs. I turned towards the dark corridor which clearly led to the back entrance of the house. I began to run into the darkness, guided by the night air, which was now flooding in from an open door. I turned and stepped out of the house into a dark and roughly paved courtyard.

Somehow I found my way through

an iron gate and into the street. I saw tall houses, closely set, traffic, horses, carriages, passersby. I began to run along the street. I did not know which way. Any way, I thought, so long as I was escaping from the jailers and their threatening prison.

My head began to throb with an overwhelming pain, but I forced myself forward. I noted night watchmen with their flares and ladies of the night soliciting customers. The stones of the pavement jarred my feet, and still I made myself cover the ground. I forced myself through the anonymous streets and made myself flee into the unknown night. Only fatigue itself brought me to a halt at last. I stopped and leaned against the wall of an inn.

I heard my breath catch in my throat; I was trembling for, in spite of my disabilities, I knew that I had run a considerable way — into the heart of London. I tried to calm myself, and looked about me. I found I was on the perimeter of a street market, which was now closing down.

I saw the flares being doused as the stalls were dismantled. Unsold goods were being loaded into horsedrawn carts. I glimpsed the fading light on oranges, fabrics, gewgaws, utensils, secondhand clothing. I stood against the wall of the inn, trying to gather my strength.

Suddenly, the door of the inn was thrown open and a group of men staggered out. They still had tankards in their hands. "Drink a toast unto His Majesty, King George," they cried. "And Prinny also. Not forgetting Lord Nelson and Lady Hamilton!"

The landlord appeared at the door, and tried to reclaim his tankards. The voices roared on. Some men fell into disarray on the pavement. Two started to fight. I shrank back into the shadows to escape their attention. But I knew I must quit the wall of the inn; there was no haven for me there. I must again go forward.

I ran from the shelter of the inn

into the street market. Amidst the confusion of packing and unpacking, uncertain which way to go or what to do, I heard voices.

"Are you traveling back to East Quayling tonight?"

"But of course. We shall arrive at dawn, and from there make our way to our farm."

"Rather you than me!"

"But we enjoy the ride after the day's trading. It is no hardship to Minnie and me. The old horse loves the moonlight, also. We shall soon be home."

I looked at the young couple who were piling their cart with vegetables they had not sold. They looked stolid and reliable. I ventured to address them.

"Did you say you were traveling to East Quayling?" I heard my voice on the night air. It sounded unfamiliar and fractured.

They looked at me with surprise. "That is so, Miss." They waited, but I could not go on. I know I held on to the edge of their stall. Their voices came to me as from a distance.

"She is hurt, Josh. She is near to fainting. Hold up, Miss. Don't fall onto this filthy floor." Hands held me upright. The mists in my mind began to clear. "Please may I travel with you?" I gasped. I groped in the pocket of my dress, but my purse had gone. "I am sorry I cannot offer you . . . "

"See Josh, the collar of her dress is covered with blood. And her hair! It is matted and torn!"

"A footpad has been at her, without doubt," Josh answered. I opened my eyes to see their anxious faces peering at me. Josh, stalwart and ruddy, and Minnie, plump and comely with brown hair. "She is unescorted and in distress. Let's get her away from here before the knave returns. She wants to travel to East Quayling, and so she shall. See here, Miss, drink this."

Josh had drawn from the pocket of his breeches a leather covered flask. He held it to my lips and I drank.

The fiery liquid scorched my throat, but it helped to dispel my nausea and weakness. "Climb into the back of the cart," Minnie said. "I will cover you with this sailcloth sheeting. No one will find you now, Miss. You are safe. The ruffian who attacked you will look for you now in vain."

Within a few seconds it seemed, the packing was finished, and the cart was away, moving with a bumping yet rhythmical motion towards its destination. I felt the spirits course in my blood. The sailcloth warmed me giving me a feeling of protection. Within a few minutes, I was asleep.

★ ★ ★

When I awoke, it was dawn, and I realized that the cart had stopped. Minnie drew back the canvas covering the cart and surveyed me. She smiled, and her good nature and kindliness were revealed in her face.

13

"We are here, Miss. Near East Quayling . . . where you wanted to come. We turn off here, so we cannot take you further." She looked at me doubtfully, as I scrambled out of the cart.

"How can I thank you?" I asked. "May I know your names so that I can repay you in time?"

"That is not necessary, Miss," said Josh, who had just come from attending to his horse. "Our names are not important, and we live several miles hence, upon a small holding. We were glad to aid you, for we deplore the violence which is so prevalent at this time. We trust you will now reach your destination safely. God speed and goodbye."

Minnie added her good wishes to her husband's. I stood on the pathway and watched them depart.

I looked around me. I was in a pleasant area of fields, trees and grasses. A wide river flowed through this district; it was contained within a low parapet, and there was a riverside path beside the water. Instinctively I turned to the river, and made my way to its edge. I clung to the low wall, and watched the gray, swift flowing water.

It is not salt water, I thought. It is not the sea, or a tidal basin. I was surprised at this reflection, and shook my head. But the sight of the river calmed and helped me; I turned from the river and looked inland.

There was a village nearby, that was plain, but where I was standing there were no houses, save one. A large square domicile stood back from the river, and, since it was built on a rise in the land, it seemed to dominate the countryside.

I looked at this house intently. I looked around again, particularly at the river. I did not know why I was here, at East Quayling. I remembered that a sensation of recognition had run through me when I had heard this name mentioned in the street market. But now, as I stood on the river pathway, I did not know what I was doing there.

I thought I would approach this house, and make a civil request for information about the district, hoping to find some clue as to my whereabouts. I began to walk across the towpath, and up a wide and sloping drive.

It was then, when I began to walk, that I realized the extent of my injuries. The pain in my head began once more and my movements racked my whole body with anguish. I felt unable to stand erect, let alone carry on a sensible conversation. I reached the high and wide front door and knocked with the metal knocker. I clung to the lintel, in case I should fall.

The door was opened by a tall thin woman, who was clearly the housekeeper. To my surprise, I heard myself speak to her. "S'il vous plaît . . . aidez-moi . . . " I heard the French language lingering in the air without surprise. I know that I fell to my knees just inside the front door.

★ ★ ★

I heard someone else hasten along the hall, and bend over me. "She spoke in a foreign tongue, Miss Imelda," the housekeeper said. "What shall I do?"

"Help me to bring her in," Miss Imelda said. "Heavens, she is injured." I know that I was lifted inside the house, into the hall. Then I heard a man approach. "Evan, do you know this young lady?"

"Why no, Imelda. I have never seen her before."

"Yet she has come here, and she is badly hurt. She has had a powerful blow to the side of her head, small wonder that she is unconscious. Please help me to get her upstairs."

I felt a man's arms go around and under my body, and I was hoisted into the air. Gradually, the man called Evan transported me up the stairs.

"We will put her in the spare front bedroom, Janet," Imelda said. "Bring water, so that I can bathe her wound.

She is smaller than myself; my own nightclothes will fit her until we can make other arrangements."

I felt capable kindly hands remove my clothing; someone used warm water to sponge my head, neck and shoulders. I know that a fire was lit in the bedroom grate, but unconsciousness still blanketed me. I heard their words as through a waterside fog.

"Where did she come from and what is her errand? Her clothes smell of vegetables!"

"Yet her underwear and linen are of fine quality, edged with guipure lace. Her dress is real velvet, lined with silk. And her shoes are genuine kid."

"She is also passing attractive," the man's voice said. "I like her auburn hair and pale skin. Not more than seventeen. Eighteen at most. She will blossom out, in time, to quite a beauty!"

"Take care what you are saying, Evan," said Imelda. "You know Vinnie is jealous, and keeps you on a short rein. Don't ask for trouble in that quarter, or you will receive it."

I then heard laughter fading away, and I sank once more into the total blackness of unconsciousness. But I knew that I did not know who I was, where I had come from, or what my destination might be.

★ ★ ★

When I had recovered some of my wits, it was to find the doctor beside my bed. I knew that he was a doctor from his trim whiskers, black coat and leather bag. He was speaking to someone just outside my line of vision.

"I trust she may remain where she is until she is well enough to speak and tell us who she is, and something of her history."

"I have questioned her, and her state of self-forgetfulness is genuine," he said. "The blow on the side of her head has inhibited her memory. We must allow nature to take its course, and restore her in a natural space of time."

"You mean she does not know who she is, Doctor Hedges? Or the circumstances of her life?"

"That is so, Miss Imelda. Her memory has quite gone. We can only hope for the best and believe that this condition is temporary. I will call again, but in the meantime . . . " The voices diminished as the doctor left the room.

I opened my eyes, and beheld one of the most arrestingly attractive women I have ever seen standing at the foot of my bed.

She had a wealth of mahogany hair which coiled freely around her face and head. Her colour was deep, her eyes an unusual shade of brandy-brown. Her figure was full and statuesque, without being stately or portentous. Her dress was casual, a little artistic. When she smiled, I saw that her teeth were small and white as alabaster. Her voice was low, but full of unexpected cadences.

"So you are awake! Welcome back to life! I am Imelda Terry, and this is my home, Riverside House. You have suffered an accident, and have been advised to rest. I am happy to offer you temporarily, the hospitality of my home."

"I cannot trespass on your kindness," I replied. "I must be up and on my way." But when I tried to get out of bed, I found that I could not move. Imelda watched with kindly amusement. Just then, a young man entered the room.

He was tall and slim, rather elegant in his movements; his hair was fair, his features even and well-proportioned. "And this is my brother, Evan," Imelda said. "We share this home. I think he will not wish you to depart too soon."

Evan laughed, and crossed to my bedside. He took my hand in his, and bowed in a formal salute. "And now you know my name," he said. "May I ask if you remember yours?"

Through the mists of my mind, the answer came. I heard myself say, "Celeste. My name is Celeste." But of any other designation I had no recollection at all.

★ ★ ★

I was in a wonderfully pleasant room; though the furniture was not new, it was tasteful and well arranged. From the windows I could see the winding river, the water grasses, the fields, and the towpath. The sky was high and wide, with rounded clouds and a vivid expanse of blue.

Soon I was well enough to walk about the room. Janet brought me my meals upon a tray, and Imelda and Evan visited me frequently. At the end of the week Dr. Hedges pronounced that I was well enough to come downstairs. I at once asked Imelda if I could depart, as I was very conscious of my status, and had no wish to be an uninvited guest for any longer than was necessary.

"Do not be in such a hurry to leave us," Imelda told me. "We are not such bores, surely? And, truth to tell I am consumed with curiosity about you. I want to know who you are, and what your background is. So wait awhile, Celeste, and do not chafe at the delay. I am sure that circumstances will reveal the truth to us, in time."

With this I had to be content. But, in honesty, I was glad to be able to rest in this agreeable place, and I already felt considerable respect and liking for my two benefactors.

When I first ventured downstairs, Evan assisted me, and we managed the stairs together. I was by now deeply interested to view the rest of the interior of Riverside House.

It was a large establishment, but now I could see clearly that the furnishings and fittings were past their best. It was as if someone with taste and money had furnished it years ago, and gradually, it had been allowed to run down.

The marquetry of the French furniture was dull and without gloss, the brocade curtains frayed and scuffed, the carpets worn and faded. Imelda and her brother lived alone here, attended only by a few faithful retainers.

Soon I was able to walk about on my own, to read, and to undertake a little sewing. I found that I could converse easily on everyday topics, but on deeper matters of my history and circumstances, I had no thoughts at all.

This must be a voyage of discovery for me, I told myself. Not only to recover my memory, but in the process to discover myself. Not only to find out who I was, but what my proclivities were, my tastes, my nature and my outlook.

I therefore set my face to the future, trusting that in time nature would aid me, and so much that was now hidden, would be revealed.

Evan soon encouraged me to leave the house. We took a short walk to the edge of the water. "Celeste, this is the River Wandle," he told me. "We are in Surrey, did you know? Lord Nelson lives quite near, just down the river, at Merton. The whole countryside considers it an honour that he choses to live in our midst."

At the end of ten days, I felt much better, and the wound upon my head was beginning to heal. Imelda had carefully arranged my reddish hair to cover the contusion and the savage bruises on my neck. Again I asked to be allowed to leave, so as not to be a burden upon their hospitality.

"Do not mention this matter further, Celeste," Imelda replied. "I like your presence here. You are no trouble, and I enjoy your company. I have no sister, and I like having a woman friend within the household; you are an admirable confidante, and I am greatly in need of the counsel of one I can trust at the present time."

I wondered what could be the cause of Imelda's concern, but did not, of course, press her for her confidences. I guessed that in some way her future was not secure, and I suddenly thought that I would do everything I could to help her find her future path.

Evan not only assisted me, but also set himself to charm me. We played bezique, he read to us in his pleasing baritone voice. He was a raconteur and charmed us with his stories. He did not work, and seemed to have no source of income, and I could not help but wonder how he supported himself in his favourite pastime.

"He is a gambler, Celeste, did you know? I am breaching no confidences in telling you this, for Evan knows of my disapproval and concern," Imelda said. "All his excitement in life depends upon the turn of a card, the racing of horses, and the throw of dice. He moves in society richer than his own. Heaven knows what his future will be when I am gone!

"I am engaged to be married, could you guess?" Imelda asked me. It was as if she wanted to discuss her betrothal, as if something was worrying her about it. "My fiancé is Robin Marchmant of Claremont Hall, an establishment set back from the River Wandle. Robin lives there with his sister, Vinnie; Vinnie and Evan are trembling on the brink of a declaration. Vinnie disapproves of Evan's propensity for gambling as well. But she has a sharp and waspish tongue, she can give him what for!

"It is rather convenient, is it not? Two brothers and sisters living so close, and brought up from childhood to be friends?" Yet she shook her head doubtfully, as if uncertain of the circumstances and the wisdom of the arrangement.

Within a few days, Imelda proposed to take me to Claremont Hall, to meet her fiancé. On a pleasant afternoon in Spring we set out in an open carriage, behind the comfortable, jogging grey mare. The elderly coachman doubled as a gardener, and had been in the Terry family's service for many years.

As we drove through the village of East Quayling, I looked with interest at the neat houses set in rows, the gardens, the winding footpaths, the ancient church. So this was where I had been so anxious to come! I thought. I pondered again the strange circumstances which had made me seek out this Surrey village as my destination. As we passed the village inn, I saw that this was captioned simply, The Hero.

"The Hero," I repeated to Imelda. "What a strange name for an inn. What does this represent?"

Imelda looked at me with surprise. "Lord Nelson, of course," she answered. "Where have you been Celeste, not to know that? Lord Nelson is our national hero, there is no need for any amplification. He is revered as the most celebrated personality of our time.

"He lived for some time *en famille*

at Merton with Sir William and Lady Hamilton. But some say it was a *ménage-à-trois*," said Imelda, and she looked at me carefully as if judging my reaction to this.

Imelda often peppered her conversation with these French words and phrases and watched my reaction. Sometimes she spoke to me in French, and I know that instinctively, I replied in French also.

For I knew now that I was bilingual, that French was as much a mother tongue to me as English. Sometimes I translated remarks into French first, before I replied in English. But what this indicated, I would not allow myself to consider, and certainly not, at this stage, to acknowledge.

"He was born in Norfolk of a clerical family," Imelda resumed, clearly still speaking about Lord Nelson. "He went to sea at the age of twelve, and his rise was meteoric.

"Cadiz, Naples, the West Indies, this country owes him so much, yet they say he has only his naval pay. Since the death of Sir William Hamilton, Lord Nelson and Lady Hamilton have shared the home. Of course Lord Nelson's marriage ended some time ago."

Imelda was talking about Lord Nelson, but her thoughts were clearly elsewhere. I looked about me with interest as we approached Claremont Hall.

That this was a well run and prosperous place was clear to see. The house was old, set amid rolling downs, and, clearly, extensive farming activities were going on in the distance, and well removed from the house. Dogs ran out to welcome us and there were stables beyond. Obviously there was money available for upkeep here. I could not help but remember Riverside House, and the deficiencies there.

Robin Marchmant was of medium height, broadly built but agile and precise in his movement. He had a rather ruddy complexion, with hazel eyes that were very searching in their regard. His hair was brown, touched at the roots with auburn, and his moustache showed traces of auburn also. His smile was friendly, but independent, and his attitude was courteous and outgoing. I liked him immediately.

He greeted me kindly, and enquired about my disabilities, for clearly Imelda had told him much about me. But his eyes were for Imelda only. When the pleasantries were over, he held her arms within his hands, and kissed her with great affection upon the cheek.

Imelda flushed and averted her eyes. I saw that she was now wearing her engagement ring, a large affair of rubies and emeralds in a cluster. Robin then showed us into the salon, a vast room which overlooked the green meadows and the farms beyond. A maidservant brought in tea.

The engaged couple then began to mention matters which were no concern of mine, and I was glad to slip out of the conversation for a few moments. I could not help but wonder what it was that caused Imelda concern in her relations with Robin.

That Robin Marchmant was in love with Imelda, was plain to see. Although he was civil and pleasant to me, his thoughts were obviously focused on Imelda, and all of his conversation revolved around her.

He was a man of honour and integrity; that was evident. What he could offer her much in worldly goods was apparent also. I wondered what it could be that held them apart, and held Imelda in this state of suspension concerning her engagement.

"She will not set our marriage day, Celeste," Robin said to me at last, with a rueful smile. "Can you prevail upon her to set a date? We are all in readiness for her here at Claremont Hall. The servants love her, and Vinnie accepts her. What can be the reason for the delay?"

"I would like to see Evan settled,"

said Imelda at last. But that was not the actual reason, I thought.

"Evan is a difficult person to plan for," Robin answered firmly. "And surely, if he becomes betrothed to Vinnie, that will aid him to find a purpose in life?"

He thought for a few moments, and then addressed Imelda again. "If it will help, I will offer to take Evan into my concern, here at Claremont Hall.

"He could train as a farm manager or a land agent. Vinnie would like that; she is often distressed by his lack of occupation. Yes, that is what I will do, Imelda, I will see Evan and make this offer to him."

But at this moment, before any further remarks could be made, the door of the room opened, and Vinnie Marchmant entered the salon.

I saw that Vinnie was rather short in stature, but that she made up for her lack of inches by her imperious stance, and the high and rather haughty angle at which she carried her head.

Her hair was like Robin's, brown with a touch of chestnut red; her skin was evenly coloured and flawless in texture. Her eyes were black, but made larger and more lustrous by long lashes upon which she had, in London fashion, smeared a liberal application of oil.

"My pleasure to see you, Imelda," she said courteously to her prospective sister-in-law. She inclined her head formally to myself but uttered no words of welcome or acknowledgement.

"I returned from Bath only last evening," Vinnie told Imelda. "So I have been unable to visit you at Riverside House. How is Evan? He is coming to dinner this evening. Will you join us, Imelda? And Miss — er-er — of course."

"Celeste," said Imelda with a slight tone of reproof. "Thank you, but no, Vinnie. I am sure you and Evan will wish to be alone."

"It is true that we have much to discuss," replied Vinnie. She had coloured slightly at Evan's name. An awkward pause seemed to fall upon the conversation.

It was at this moment that a sensation of faintness overcame me; these spasmodic attacks assailed me at times. I turned to Imelda and asked her if I might excuse myself from the company for a moment, to give my disquieted nerves time to recover.

At once, Robin and Imelda were solicitous. Imelda insisted on escorting me to a small anteroom nearby, where there was a chaise longue. Robin fetched me a small draught of cognac. I begged them to return to the salon, and to leave me to rest for a while, alone. The parlour maid was instructed to wait outside the anteroom door, to attend to my needs. I was glad finally to be alone.

It was then I heard footsteps outside in the carpeted corridor beyond the door, which had been left ajar. I heard voices.

"What are you doing here, Deborah?

Why are you stationed outside the anteroom door?"

"The young lady with Miss Imelda has come over faint, and is resting on the chaise. 'Tis the young French lady, who is staying at Riverside House, Mrs. Johnson."

"A curse upon the French," replied Mrs. Johnson, who was clearly the housekeeper. "We can do without them in England. What use is it Lord Nelson confronting the French, if we have them on our doorsteps in East Quayling?"

"Oh, Mrs. Johnson she is not like that at all. She speaks English the way you or I do. They are all here, Mrs. Johnson." Deborah lowered her voice. "All except Mr. Evan, and he's practicing with the dice, so the coachman says."

"I know who is here, Deborah," replied Mrs. Johnson. "Since I baked for the tea. I shall be pleased, without doubt, to have some finality in this matter of future arrangements. I cannot understand the delay. It is a wonderfully good arrangement. Why don't they accept their good fortune before Fate intervenes? Miss Imelda could come here as mistress, and Miss Vinnie go to Riverside House.

"It would be an exchange of benefits all around. Miss Vinnie could take her own money to Riverside House, for heaven knows it needs refurbishing, and Mr. Evan needs ready cash. And, Miss Imelda could enjoy Mr. Robin's money as mistress of Claremont Hall. What more can mortals ask or want?"

I heard smothered laughter, and then I heard footsteps retreating. I knew that Deborah remained at her post alone.

It certainly seemed a very good arrangement, as outlined by Mrs. Johnson, I thought, as I rose from the chaise longue. However, life does not always allocate things out so evenly.

I was beginning to believe that Evan was less than keen on Vinnie, and that he was becoming attracted to myself;

in return, my friendship was deepening for him.

Robin loved Imelda, but Imelda was not certain of her feelings for him. The pot was on the boil, I thought. Who could know what would come out? But what came out in the end mightily surprised us all.

# 2

I MUST admit that Evan's friendship meant much to me in the following days, for he set himself out to further our relationship. It was thanks to his efforts that my general health improved and I began to recover my energy and strength.

Yet my memory did not return, and the whole of my earlier life remained a blank to me.

I grieved continually, naturally, that the members of my family must be disturbed by my disappearance. I had vanished from somewhere. Someone must be in despair about my absence. I longed to be in touch with those I had cared for, but when I stretched out my arms in the empty night, there was nothing and nobody. But thoughts of my new 'family' also kept me occupied.

Evan's style of living continued to baffle and amaze me. He had no gainful occupation, yet he was always busy, and never bored. He rode, he visited friends, he wrote letters, he played cards, he rolled the dice. He loved the River Wandle and walked along the towpath often. It was a life which gave him enjoyment. Yet, to his family and friends, his life appeared wasted and without gain of any kind; his lack of ambition and direction clearly angered Vinnie.

She visited us early after my visit to Claremont Hall. We sat in the conservatory which adjoined the drawing room. Vinnie said to Evan:

"And what transpired during your visit to London, Evan. Did you see your uncle?"

"I called to see him, but he was absent."

"And where was Lord Stanhope, may I ask?"

"In Venice."

"Venice? At this time of the year?"

Vinnie looked at Evan sceptically. It was clear that she did not believe that Evan had visited his uncle. "So you are no nearer to obtaining a position," she said. "What about Robin's offer?"

"Really Vinnie, can you see me engaged in agriculture? Please leave this matter in abeyance. Time will solve everything for me. There is no need to fret ourselves now."

"You visited gaming houses in London, I suppose, Evan. And other social gatherings of a dubious nature."

"Do not be so censorious, Vinnie! I bet on the tables at Bucks. I showed a handsome profit. It is always possible to make money from games of chance, if one knows how."

I excused myself from the room, for it was clear that some altercation was about to take place between Evan and Vinnie. When Vinnie had gone Evan sought me out.

"I must apologize for Vinnie's behaviour," he said. "She appears more stringent than she actually is, though truth to tell, I suppose she has some grounds for her complaints.

"Lord Stanhope is not only my uncle but was, earlier in my life, my guardian. He is immensely rich and is also a celebrated reformer. Have you heard of him, Celeste?"

I shook my head. Evan continued, "He is unmarried without family, save for Imelda and myself. It is expected that in time Imelda will marry Robin, and I shall become the sole heir of my uncle. But . . . " Here Evan paused and looked at me doubtfully, as if wondering how I was receiving this information. " . . . my uncle disapproves of the type of activities which make up my life. He hates gambling, racing, riotous company and the general social scene in certain circles in London. I have to hide much from him. I enjoy my rather unconventional friendships, but I know my uncle would condemn them. It is a difficult thing, sometimes, to keep my proclivities from his notice."

We both paused, then I said, "But surely your uncle would look with favour upon your obtaining normal occupation, Evan. You could become a notary, for example." I knew that Evan was quick to assimilate facts, and had a retentive mind.

"Please do not join the ranks of my persecutors, Celeste," he replied earnestly, yet with a smile. "Everyday occupation is an anathema to me. So long as I can scrape by upon my own courses, I will."

In my bed in the bedroom which overlooked the River Wandle, I would lie awake and ponder my predicament. The past was a blank, and yet sometimes flashes of memory shot across the darkness of my recollection.

I could see the reflection of water on the ceiling of another room, hear footsteps upon the cobbles stones of a quay, hear men's voices and the sounds of some maritime activity. I was in a port, but where this was, I did not know.

I sensed also the kindly presence of a family. There was a settled homely scene, warmth, kindliness and affection. But who were the people who had given this to me in my life? I did not know.

I was also deeply concerned about my continued presence in the Terry household. Monetary matters must be pressing for them; yet they would not hear of my leaving their home. I made up my mind to repay them doublefold, when I had recovered my memory, and the circumstances of my life had been revealed.

In the meantime, I busied myself about Riverside House. "These curtains," I ventured to say to Imelda, "if one stitched a row of braid to the edges, this would cover the fraying and improve the whole. Also the cushion cases. A little appliqué work would hide the tears, and make them almost like new."

"How kind you are, Celeste," Imelda replied. "I am hopeless with a needle.

What small stitches! You work the continental fashion, Celeste. And your appliqué! That is all the rage in Paris. You are a marvellous addition to the household. What would I do without you, my dear?"

We sat together in her small boudoir, which adjoined her bedroom. I was sewing, but Imelda appeared ill at ease. It was clear she wished to speak to me.

"I know you approve of my engagement to Robin," she began. "And I approve it myself, for I love Robin with all my heart. But a grievous circumstance has arisen which is likely to rend us apart."

She paused, then resumed. "Some time ago, when I was young, I had a fall from a horse. I thought nothing of the matter until recently, when I began to have internal pain.

"While I was visiting my uncle, in London, I went privately to see a doctor skilled in these matters. He examined me in the presence of a nurse, and told me that I had certain internal displacements, and that I should never bear a child. Frankly, I was astounded, and deeply disturbed. For I know that Robin longs for a family, and is anxious to have a son, an heir to his lands and possessions. Vinnie has money of her own and Robin has no wish to bequeath his inheritance to his sister. His only other heirs are remote cousins. Robin therefore looks forward to our family, and to having a male child to carry on the line."

Imelda got up and walked to the window of the little room. I saw her voluptuous figure, the charming disarray of her chestnut hair, her general air of generosity and amplitude. Her personality was vibrant, as always; it filled the very air we breathed. She turned to me.

"Of course, I cannot tell Robin this," she said. "It would not be acceptable to mention such intimate matters between us. I could not bring myself to say the words, and I do not know how Robin

46

would receive it in any case; I could not bare to see his rejection or distaste."

I laid down my stitching. I know that I looked at her with amazement. "But we are all human beings, Imelda," I cried. "Surely Robin would not be averse to hearing the truth. Certainly you must feel you can mention such a matter to him, since you are engaged, and are expected to wed soon!"

"Perhaps where you come from, Celeste, the atmosphere is more liberal, and this is possible. But I assure you that now, in England at the present time, such a conversation between a man and a woman is unthinkable.

"If only I could find a way to end our engagement," she said. "If only he would dismiss me for some reason, it would solve my problem and elucidate everything. I shall never marry anyone else of course. But at least I should be spared the pain of confessing my inadequacy. This is pain I cannot face, and will never endure, for my love makes this pain doubly hard to sustain. It is indeed love which adds the complications to our lives."

★ ★ ★

A few days after this confession, Imelda decided to give a dinner party. "Lord Stanhope is coming to stay," she informed me. "And I wish to invite some local dignitaries, to meet him. Could you prepare a crême chantilly, Celeste? I love your continental dishes. And Lord Stanhope is much traveled and appreciates good cuisine."

I was only too willing to assist, and was busy in the kitchen all morning, and in the dining room sorting out silver canteen.

Before luncheon, Imelda asked me to accompany her upstairs, and into a bedroom that was little used. "I have lately gained weight," she told me frankly. "My figure was not always as generous as you see it now. Consequently, I have a wardrobe full of clothes in good condition, but which are too small. Take your pick, Celeste," she cried, swishing aside the curtain of a small recess. I saw a whole collection of stylish and slimfitting clothes before me.

I remonstrated, but with little effect. Reluctantly, yet with good grace, I accepted her kindly offer. And indeed, I had no choice but to do so, for my one and only velvet dress was now becoming well worn, and the laundering of my linen and hose each evening was becoming a problem. I also did not wish to disgrace Imelda at the dinner party that night.

During the afternoon, when the preparations were well advanced, I excused myself to Imelda and strolled down to the River Wandle. Truth to tell, the exertions had tired me, and had brought on a resumption of the pain in my neck and shoulder. I hoped for a few moments of quiet in which to compose myself before it was time to dress. I leaned on the escarpment of the river and looked out over the shining water.

As always, the river calmed me. How I loved the waters of the seas, I thought. Even this fresh water river was a blessing.

In the distance I could see the local fishermen arranging their lines and bait. There was quite a lot of local fishing nearby, and the voices of the men came to me clearly. I watched the clouds riding high, and the sunlight fractured by the water. Then I heard a footstep, and I turned my head to see a young man approaching along the path which ran beside the water.

He was tall and dark, with a little peaked cap upon his head. He wore moleskin trousers, and the long thigh boots of a fisherman. His navy blue jacket was well-worn; it was open to reveal the gansey of a crewman. He had a kerchief at his neck with a nautical knot. I noted that his stride was long and purposeful.

To my surprise, this young man did not continue along the towpath, and pass me upon the embankment, but turned and mounted the steps which led to the private driveway of Riverside House. He nodded to me civilly, and then began to make his way towards the gates which led to the front of the house. I thought it my duty to speak to him. I turned and hastened after him.

"Excuse me, sir," I said. "Is there something you require from Riverside House?"

The young man stoped and regarded me. I saw that his eyes were grey, direct and searching in their regard, as are the eyes of all seamen, but without presumption or discourtesy. He did not reply, as if the question and my presence had surprised him.

"If you require the tradesmen's entrance," I continued, "that is further along this promenade. This path whereupon you now stand is private, and leads to the front door and the conservatory of the house."

The young man bowed his head. "I regret ma'am, if my presence here displeases you. I did not intend to trespass and intrude. I will, as you advise, retrace my footsteps. Good day Miss, and a thousand apologies."

I watched him go. Contrary to my expectations, he did not make his way to the back of the house where tradesmen were expected, but continued to stride along the towpath. I watched his retreating figure. I felt strangely perplexed and at a loss.

There was something about his remarks, his phrasing and his tone that surprised me. He had given me a final rather mocking bow, and his eyes had glimmered with amusement. The whole encounter puzzled me and I was filled with unease.

I returned to the house. Vinnie had arrived, and was arranging a centrepiece of flowers for the table. Imelda said:

"I had asked Judge Stanley to dinner, but he has sent a message that he cannot attend, owing to legal duties in London. He has asked me instead to receive his son, Miles, who is on leave from his ship, the *Victory*. I have agreed, and have sent Miles a formal invitation for this evening.

"I expected to receive a messenger with an acceptance. No doubt it will arrive later. Please keep the centrepiece low in design, Vinnie," Imelda added. "I do not want the guests to be hemmed in and lost in foliage."

"It is a long time since I saw Miles Stanley," Evan said reflectively.

"That is not unremarkable, since he spends so much of his time at sea. The *Victory* is Lord Nelson's flagship. I am told that Miles has his confidence and is well regarded by Lord Nelson and other officers.

"It would do you good to go to sea, Evan," his sister resumed. "The discipline would calm you and a career would give you direction. You are wasting your time and have nothing to show for your days."

"He will not quit the social scene in London," said Vinnie tartly, as she tugged at a sprig of conifer. "You must be careful Evan, not to offend your uncle this evening."

"I am well aware of my responsibilities," said Evan. He was already sampling the wine. He smiled at me, but I thought there was an undercurrent of seriousness in his remark.

"Miles Stanley is the most eligible young man in the county, Celeste," said Imelda. "His father is a baronet, but prefers to be known simply as Judge Stanley. Many other men have titles, greater wealth, more social prominence. Yet somehow, in some way, Miles Stanley tops them all. He is the most sought after man in Surrey. Many mammas have their eyes upon him for their daughters."

I made no reply, for in some strange way the praise of this paragon was making me defensive against him. No doubt he will be conceited, I thought, and full of self-importance. He will be stout and bald and reek of tar and gunpowder. I decided that the matchmaking in Surrey did not concern me at all.

"Yes, many women have sought to catch Miles Stanley in their net," Imelda went on. "Without result. Yet it is not for want of trying, is it Vinnie?" Imelda resumed in a teasing tone. She turned to me, "Vinnie was greatly smitten with Miles Stanley before she turned her attentions to Evan. Something went wrong, did it not Vinnie? The affaire did not work out. But one must not mention these things. Forgive me if I overstep the mark, Vinnie. I trust it will not cause you pain to see Miles Stanley again."

"I pardon your remarks, Imelda, but they are out of place. My friendship with Miles is over. Please do not refer to it again."

I saw Vinnie's hands tremble as she tried to push a flower stem into the water of the crystal vase. I saw also that her expression was forced and strange, and I thought that her affection for this Miles Stanley was still not over, while her relationship with Evan was also in flux.

No wonder she was often distant and abrupt; her whole life seemed to lack certainty within herself and from others. Her life was built on shifting sands in which there was no basis of acceptance or commitment. I was not surprised to see tears stand in her eyes.

I went to my room to change. I had chosen to wear a dress of corn-coloured silk with a bodice of gold lace. It was cut rather low, and I did not have Imelda's expansive bosom to fill it out. Yet when I was ready, I looked into the mirror, and was not displeased with the reflection.

My auburn hair had grown over the wound on my head, and my settled and happy life at Riverside House had brought colour to my cheeks and brightness to my blue eyes. I saw my figure was trim and shapely; the bruises on my neck and shoulder had faded. A sudden wave of optimism swept over me. I looked forward to the evening and the assembly of the guests. Perhaps soon my life would develop, and I would see my way ahead. I felt I was about to advance from darkness into light.

I descended the stairs, and entered the drawing room, where the family and guests had assembled. I saw that Imelda looked her usual lavish and dramatic self, dressed in a flowing gauze cape which fell around the shoulders of her green brocade dress. Vinnie wore a trim outfit of pale silver. The other local notables wore their best; the gentlemen had been lavish with their medals and decorations.

I was surprised to find that I did not recognize any of these ornaments. It seemed that the history of this area was unknown to me. I was still a stranger in a strange place. But I put all such thoughts away from me, and determined to do my best to help Imelda make the evening a success. I was aroused from my thoughts by Janet, who opened the drawing room door, and announced,

"Lieutenant Miles Stanley."

Something in Janet's tone alerted me. It was clear that the bearer of this name found favour in her eyes; her tone was cordial, even excited. I turned to see this notability, for at the mention of this name it seemed all the occupants of the room were also alerted, and composed themselves to welcome the newcomer.

I saw a tall, dark young man dressed in the white-toned trousers of a lieutenant in the navy of King George the Third; he wore a dark cutaway jacket with gold frogging and epaulettes; his linen was immaculate.

He carried his sword, since this was a formal occasion. He wore also a single badge of decoration, but again this was new to me. I did not know where he had served, or how he had received this naval honour.

He entered the room with deference towards his hostess, Imelda, yet with confidence and ease. His eyes were kindly and humorous as they swept over the assembled company. Lieutenant Stanley was plainly used to social occasions, and would make a polished contribution to the evening.

Yet I knew there was more to this young man than this formal figure attending a soirée. I had seen him only that morning dressed in the working kit of a ship's crewman. I had seen the gansey, the sailcloth trousers, the capable hands scorched from ropes, the long legs that could scale a rigging. And in that moment I knew that Miles Stanley would never ask any seaman to do what he himself could not do.

He was bowing to me as we were presented. He gave no indication that we had met previously, but the memory of the young seaman on the towpath seemed burned into my mind. He had arrived with some impact in my life, and I guessed that this impact would grow, and not diminish.

# 3

IMELDA had adopted the newest London custom of serving a small glass of wine while the guests assembled before dinner. Some thought this strange, yet I approved. (Perhaps this was done where I came from.) It helped the general conversation and prepared a convivial attitude towards the meal ahead.

After the presentation of Lieutenant Stanley to myself, Imelda said, "Please sit side by side, and talk to one another. You are strangers now, but we must remedy this." We each accepted a glass of wine, and regarded each other. It seemed that we had no use for formalities or hedging. I said to the Lieutenant, directly:

"You deceived me this afternoon, sir, as to your identity. I think you owe me an explanation concerning this."

"Believe me ma'am, I did not deceive you," Miles Stanley answered earnestly. "You deceived yourself."

"Your clothing led me to the wrong conclusion about your status, sir," I answered with spirit. "I cannot be blamed for that."

"I do not apportion blame to anyone, Miss Celeste," Lieutenant Stanley answered. "I often wear the working clothes of a crewman when I am home on leave. This gives me informality, yet still links me with the sea."

I saw now that his hair was not as dark as I had first thought. It was tinged with fairer strands, which lightened the whole. His eyes also, were not entirely grey but were flecked with blue; his features were even, a little aquiline, his mouth precise yet mobile. He could grant a compliment to a lady, yet give a command to a seaman which would be obeyed.

"You care greatly for the sea, then, sir," I added, to bridge the pause.

"Indeed yes. The sea attracted me

from my childhood, and I saw no future for myself save in its service."

"I too love the sea," I said.

And this was true. The sea drew me as a magnet, as a vista once loved and lost, as a dream of home.

Suddenly, Miles Stanley began to talk to me about the characteristics of the various seas he had encountered. Of the rollers of the Atlantic, the choppy currents of La Manche, the smooth tricky undercurrents of the Baltic waters.

But before I could reply, Imelda intervened. "Please enter the dining room on the arm of Evan, Celeste, and Miles shall escort Vinnie. But never fear, you will be close to one another, you four, and can continue to discuss the matters which interest you." So saying, she began to shepherd the company into the dining room. The scene which met our eyes amply repaid the household for their efforts.

Polished silver shone upon white nappery; Vinnie's centrepiece drew all eyes. The chandelier above the table glowed softly; its brilliants had been repaired and polished.

Lord Stanhope had arrived earlier, and had been presented to the company as the guest of the evening. He was invited to take the head of the table. The local worthies were indeed delighted to meet such a celebrated figure. Lord Stanhope responded with deference and charm, giving to the Mayor of East Quayling and his lady, and other local guests, the respect he clearly thought their achievements merited.

Evan also made much of his uncle, which was to be expected, since all his hopes were based on Lord Stanhope. Was he also hoping to effect a loan? I wondered, for I knew Evan had recently been short of money, and that the dice had not fallen his way. He was obliged to finance his way of life from somewhere, I reflected, but Lord Stanhope did not seem like an easy man to deceive. I guessed that gambling debts did not come within the scope of his philanthropic activities.

Lord Stanhope himself had surprised me. I had expected a puritan figure, an elderly reformer who disapproved of mankind and human frailties. Yet his lordship could not have been more than fifty. He was of medium height with a fresh face and beautifully coiffed gray hair; his eyes were blue and observant. His attitude was courtly but without affectation, and he clearly liked his fellowmen, while deploring man of their proclivities. He began to talk about his activities.

"There is so much to be done," he said, "before this land of ours is fit to live in. Many areas need reform; there are women working on dungheaps, children abandoned, appalling poverty, gin palaces, the exploitation of old soldiers and seamen. And now, a new area of scandal has come to my notice.

"Children and young women have been abducted to work in bordellos.

I understand that this is a new fetish among some men-about-town. Young females are forced into submission, into degrading practices. This goes beyond prostitution, since the female participants are young and defenseless, and have no redress or means of escape.

"Something must be done. I am making these appalling houses my next target for dissolution. I intend to bend all my energies to discovering and closing these establishments. The Bow Street magistrates have promised to aid me in my work, if I can but discover where these dens are situated."

I laid down my fork, for at Lord Stanhope's words, a strange sensation assailed me. I remembered the blow upon my head, my awakening in the dank and malodorous rear quarters of some unknown commercial enterprise, my flight from the room, the pause as I surveyed the foyer of the house, the smell of stale human beings, sweat, perfume, pain.

I remembered that I had heard distant cries; the place had been alive with human activity. Voices had been heard, shrieks of protest, the sounds of stultifying torment. The images receded. I found that I was trembling and that my hands were damp with perspiration.

I saw also, in a sudden flash of hindsight, the young man who had stood in the entrance to this establishment. I saw his evening clothes, his long opera cloak with the crimson lining, the silver-topped cane. But more than this, I saw his figure and form, his head and his features, and my realization of who this was made me close to fainting. I closed my eyes, and willed the images to recede from my mind.

I realized that a hand had closed over mine, and that anxious eyes regarded me. I heard Miles Stanley's voice as from a distance, "May I assist you, Miss Celeste? A small sip of wine will aid you; you have been busy all day, I know, helping Imelda. And you are not yet fully recovered from your accident."

He continued to hold my hand within his sure clasp, as he raised the wineglass towards me. I took the crystal glass from his hand, and looked at him with gratitude. It was as if he knew my malaise had deep roots in the past, and that he was aiding me to recover my poise, and to accept my life and circumstances in the present and future.

All embarrassment was spared me by the conversation, for the subject of Lord Nelson had been broached, and it seemed that all tongues were awag.

"It is true this country owes him an immeasurable debt," the local notary was saying. "He has not only won prime victories for England in many theatres of war, but has been an unofficial ambassador for England in many lands. His diplomacy in the West Indies was notable indeed."

"It was in the West Indies that he

married Mrs. Nesbit. She was a widow with a child," his wife was adding. "I understand that the marriage was not a happy one, though it was rumoured she did all she could for his aid and comfort. But somehow . . . " the lady shrugged . . . "she failed to please."

"It was after the breakdown of his marriage, or it could have been before . . . " the lady dithered, "at any rate, Lord Nelson joined his fortunes to the Hamiltons. Lord Nelson has no children of his own from his marriage to Mrs. Nesbit. Only a stepson, who does not win his promotion in the navy upon merit. He is an obnoxious boy, I am told. Though Lord Nelson does all he can to aid this recalcitrant youth."

I saw that Miles was about to refute some of these rather sweeping statements, but before he could get a word in edgeways, Vinnie said:

"But there is a child at Merton. A little girl. Her parentage is a matter of speculation."

"This young child," said Miles

stoutly, "was given into Lord Nelson's charge in Italy, and he entrusted the small orphan into Lady Hamilton's keeping. It is to her ladyship's credit that she undertook the responsibility. I have this assurance of good authority. Indeed, Lord Nelson told me the truth of his matter, himself."

There was silence at Miles' defense of his captain, but incredulity and doubt were reflected upon many faces. It was clear that the child was considered as belonging to Lord Nelson and Lady Hamilton. I wondered what had been the reactions, and what part the husband, Sir William, had played in this strange situation. I did not know that I should eventually find out.

Vinnie sat on the other side of Miles, and she soon engaged him in earnest conversation. But during a lull in their discourse, I ventured to ask the lieutenant: "For how long is your leave, sir? Must you soon rejoin your ship?"

"Eventually, Miss Celeste, when the

admiralty sends me my signal. But before that arrives I have another commission to fulfill. I have been ordered to Portsmouth to take an advanced instruction in weaponry. For it is the guns and ammunition that I am concerned with on the *Victory*. It is essential that, when Lord Nelson gives the order to attack, the guns are not only poised upon the target, but are fully provisioned with shot and gunpowder, and manned by teams both alert and experienced.

"Wish me good fortune, please, upon this enterprise! I trust we shall marry theory with practice and obtain a practical and forceful outcome from these deliberations. I know Lord Nelson relies upon me in this, and I am anxious to serve him well at all times."

I looked at Miles Stanley's face as he spoke these words. He was an obviously dedicated and proficient weaponry officer. I would not allow myself to think of the danger wherein he stood, in his commission aboard the

*Victory*. To silence the enemies' guns was the first order of an opposing navy, and I knew that casualties were high in naval battles, and that the decks around the guns were sanded so that men should not slip in their own and their companion's blood.

I did not wonder how I knew these details; I accepted these occasional revelations of my past in the hope that more would be revealed, and that, eventually, new light would shine upon my situation and upon my former life.

"It has been a pleasure to talk to you, Miss Celeste," Miles Stanley said, and for a moment his hand brushed mine upon the damask cloth. I coloured instantly, for somehow the touch of his hand affected me deeply. And I knew that I liked this young naval officer intensely; he awoke deep chords within me. His personality was so open, yet complex, so sophisticated, yet so honourable, I responded to him as a flower to the sun, or a moth to a flame.

The meal drew to a close, and the ladies withdrew, to leave the gentlemen with their port wine. Vinnie sought me out at once.

"Do not be too taken with Miles, Celeste," she said. "Many young ladies have been affected by him. He has shown a passing interest, but this interest has waned, and they have been left high and dry. He is wedded to the sea, and cares deeply for no woman. I would not like to see you disappointed, and hurt."

I knew that Vinnie's comments were uttered not from solicitude, but were the product of sour grapes. But I noticed that, though she herself had been disappointed by Miles, she did not overtly pursue him, or bring herself to his notice. I gave her credit for her discretion. Sometimes Vinnie could surprise and show an unexpected side to her nature. I hoped that she would eventually find the solution to the problems that so perplexed her.

Imelda brought Lord Stanhope to my

side, and the noble gentleman engaged me in conversation. I found him to be open and agreeable, and I wondered why he had never married. But he too seemed wedded to another course. His dedication to the much needed reforms of the ills in English society at this time occupied his mind, his time, and his life. Evan joined us and chatted charmingly with his uncle.

The evening drew to a close. As Miles Stanley prepared to depart, he drew me aside.

"May I write to you from Portsmouth?" he asked me. "I guess the course may be arduous, and to be in correspondence with yourself might aid and refresh me. May I address you so, Miss Celeste?"

"Certainly, Lieutenant Stanley," I replied. A wave of pleasure, and indeed, happiness, assailed me. I know that I smiled up into his face, as his blue-grey eyes regarded me.

"I shall regard it as an honour," he said. He raised my hand to his lips, and again my whole being was deeply affected by his nearness, and the brushing of his lips upon my hand. "*Bon voyage*," I said. "And good fortune!" He smiled his thanks to me, and then was gone.

I now offered to help Imelda and Janet to finish clearance of the dining room, and the remnants of the party, but Imelda would have none of it.

"You have done so well, Celeste," she said. "You have helped to entertain the guests and everyone sings your praises. The Mayor is charmed with you, and the notary's wife wishes to ask you to call. Be off with you now, to bed. It is an order, not a request. I insist!"

She stood at the bottom of the stairs, and watched me mount upwards, towards the landing. And, truthfully, I was glad to go, for I felt weary, and there was a matter of importance, which I must be alone to think through. It was a concern of deep importance, I thought, and one which could affect the whole of my future life.

Towards the end of the evening, Miles Stanley had spoken again of the role the navy must play in the defense of England.

He had praised Lord Nelson's dedication and skill. He had spoken of the ardours of the naval crewmen to defend the country of their birth. It was clear that the British navy were preparing for a battle ahead.

"The whole navy is looking forward to engaging the French," Miles had said. "And Lord Nelson most of all."

"Lord Nelson will rally the whole country. He will lead more than the navy. He will lead the whole nation to victory over our ancient enemies, the French!"

That this was Miles' own deeply held conviction was clear. He was a man dedicated to the defense of his country. Everyone knew that England had to fight in self-defense, or be overrun by Napoleon and his hordes. It was either fight, or lose independence and a national way of life.

I undressed, put on a light robe, and crossed to the window. Outside the River Wandle shone, striped with silver in the moonlight. The willows on the banks moved a little in the breeze. Pale clouds drifted by. The guests had gone, and everything was still.

What was my own nationality? I asked myself. Where had I come from and what were my origins? Was I myself, French?

Was I an enemy alien? Was I indeed an adversary of the country which was giving me shelter, and whose people had shown towards me such kindness and affection?

I turned from the window, beginning to consider the evidence.

French came readily to my tongue and my mind, and many of my private soliloquies took place in the French language.

When I had been asked my name, I had answered "Celeste," but it had been with a French inflection. The harbour scenes which flashed into my mind had a foreign flavour, the voices an alien accent, the sounds of shoes on stone, a continental ring.

My stitching had been French, and my clothes were French also. Was I myself a French national? Was France my home, and did I owe allegiance to another power?

I felt tears flood into my eyes. If this was true, what an insurmountable barrier it was to my friendship with Miles Stanley! A man dedicated to fighting the French could hardly be expected to look with favour upon a young woman whose family ties were with the enemy.

It seemed that I had found a man I could care for and who affected me deeply, only to find a patent impediment in the way of our relationship. If I were French, I could care intensely for a man who was the enemy of my country, but I guessed that he could never bring himself to care for me.

I got into bed, but I could not sleep. I relived the events of the evening. I saw Miles' eyes upon me, felt the touch of his hand upon mine as he offered me strength and solace, and felt the tenderness of his kiss upon parting. It seemed that we must eventually part forever, yet I clung to the memory of his promise of a letter. Upon such frail hopes are dreams built, and wishes laid; I fell asleep with his name upon my lips.

Yet before I slept, I saw in cameo, a sudden flash of revelation and understanding, Evan talking with grace and attention to his Uncle, Lord Stanhope.

I saw Evan's small features, his fair hair, his style and his grace.

Then I knew that Evan was the young man I had seen in the foyer of the bordello!

# 4

THERE was no doubt but that the whole of England was preparing for the naval battle to come. But if there were battles to be waged at sea, in our small circle also there were the shifting currents of varying interest, and the clash of personalities, as each pursued his or her designated course.

I early decided to see Imelda and mention my new fear, that I must be French, and that this made my continued residence amongst dedicated anglophiles untenable. But Imelda halted me almost before I had begun.

"No one can be sure of your nationality, Celeste," she said. "There is some indication that you may be French. On the other hand, you may be an English girl who had been sent to school on the continent to gain a knowledge of languages and foreign customs. You may have been in a convent in rural France, though you do not show signs of this. You move easily in the world, Celeste. A religious retreat is not the explanation in your case.

"Your concern about your nationality relates to Miles Stanley, does it not? I saw he was taken with you, and you responded to his attentions."

Imelda did not warn me against him, as I expected. Instead she told me, "The enemy of today is the ally of tomorrow. Had Miles been concerned about your continental nationality, he would not have offered you his friendship. With this you must be content, Celeste. Do not press matters forward too fast. Bide your time until your memory returns naturally. Await this awakening, and be thankful that your injuries were no worse."

These latter words of Imelda led me to consider again my new conviction that Evan was the young man I had seen in the entrance to the house of ill-fame. Yet I felt that I could not mention this, outright, to his sister.

Also, I felt that Evan's presence on that fateful night had some other association with my life. It was not by chance that our lives were connected. Somewhere, somehow there was a logical explanation of these rather puzzling events.

"I know what you are struggling to say," Imelda said, smiling, and trying to help me. "You were greatly affected when Uncle Edmund spoke of the bordello where young women are imprisoned and exploited. You think, do you not, that it is to one of these places you were taken when you were abducted, and where you suffered your injuries?

"Do not dwell on this, Celeste. And it is useless to mention the matter to Lord Stanhope. You do not know the address of this place, do you?" I shook my head. I remembered only the long anonymous street, the traffic, the alleys glimpsed in the lamplight, the flares of the nightwatchmen, the cries of the streetwalkers, the inn, and, finally, the street market where I had met my benefactors.

"I was quite lost," I said. "I do not know where this place is situated at all." But Evan knows, I thought. And I determined to speak to Evan on this matter without delay.

"When you finally know this address, we will communicate with my uncle," Imelda told me. "And Lord Stanhope can be in touch with the magistrates. So be patient, Celeste. Matters will work out. Events have aided you so far, and they will again."

Although Imelda took time to offer me words of comfort and reassurance, I sensed that her own mind was far from quiet. She remained perplexed concerning her own private dilemma. I ventured to mention this matter to her, seeking to aid her, if I could.

"Yes, it is true," she said. "The essential matter has not changed. I am still engaged to a man who wishes for an heir, and I am unable to bear a child. What am I to do, Celeste? I see no way forward or out of this impasse."

"Would you marry Robin if he assured you that your condition made no difference to his love for you?" I asked her.

Imelda stared at me in astonishment. "However could such a thing be?"

An idea came to me. "Would you allow me to go to Robin on your behalf, and tell him the truth of this matter?" I asked.

Imelda stared at me with amazement. "You would do that? Would you, Celeste? Go to Robin and tell him . . . " Words failed her. "But I could not allow you, as a guest to discuss such intimate womanly matters with a man."

"Wherever I come from," I said, "I think that there is less veiling of essentials. I am certain that Robin would not be taken aback or offended. He has not led a sheltered life, screened from the realities of existence. I think you owe it to him to tell him the truth. Then it will be his own decision as to his future course. And yours."

"At least I would then know my fate and my future, and end this uncertainty," Imelda said. "Perhaps you are right, Celeste. Perhaps there is a lack of frankness between the sexes, today. At least, if you try, we shall soon know. For Robin is not one to beat about the bush, and will soon make his reactions known to both you and myself."

It was approaching time for luncheon, but I sped off to fetch my cloak, and Imelda alerted the coachman. With a few minutes I was on my way towards Claremont Hall, pondering my strange commission. There was no doubt there was a difference between my upbringing and English customs in these matters.

Robin had just entered the Hall from one of the farms. Naturally, he was surprised to see me. He took me into the dining room, where a cold collation was arranged on the polished

84

table. Vinnie was absent he told me, visiting in a distant village, and he was lunching alone. He indicated a chair and we were seated.

I began to speak to him earnestly, to tell him of Imelda's accident, and the consequent internal displacement. I stressed her grief to know that she could never bear his child. He heard me courteously, but with great attention. It was clear he understood my phrases and their implications entirely.

"I remember this accident well," he told me, when I had finished. "Indeed, I was present at the time. Imelda was a courageous rider, and she attempted to take a high fence. Her horse was unschooled, and she fell heavily to the ground. I myself aided her, and brought her back to Claremont Hall. Indeed, by a strange coincidence, it was at this time that I first fell in love with her, and felt a great longing to aid and succour her throughout her life, a longing and a desire which has never left me, and does not leave me now, in spite of your revelations concerning her inability to bear a child."

Robin rose to his feet, and held my hand in his. "I will myself call to see Imelda later today, and tell her my reactions to your revelations. But for your own peace of mind, I will tell you my decision now.

"It makes no difference to my love for Imelda, to know that we cannot create a family. My love goes beyond any future expectations and is based upon the person of Imelda, and Imelda alone.

"I shall insist that the wedding proceeds apace, and I trust you will attend. For we both owe you a debt Celeste. You have undertaken this mission to aid us both, and have carried it out with discretion and kindliness."

Robin raised my hand to his lips, and we smiled at one another. I felt nothing but admiration for Imelda's fiancé, and I trusted, that now this matter was settled, we might have a little plain sailing in our lives.

Robin pressed me now to take a glass of wine, and since it was long past the time for luncheon, to take a repast with him. This I did, knowing that Imelda was sure of my whereabouts. It was in a more settled frame of mine that I began the journey home.

Indeed I felt a surge of happiness at the successful conclusion to my errand. I asked the coachman to let me alight at a bend in the River Wandle. I felt that I must savour my pleasure as I walked in the open air. I turned my face with eagerness, and my step was light as I approached Riverside House.

It is at such moments, that Fate lies in wait for us. When we congratulate ourselves upon our good fortune, she prepares a hidden blow. And so it was with me, at this moment. For as I began to climb the steps from the towpath to the promenade above, I saw a figure coming down the drive of Riverside House.

The figure was that of a man,

a young man. He was fashionably dressed, though his clothes were flashy and overly ornate. He wore one of the new bowlers over his pomaded hair, and carried a malacca cane, with which he lightly whipped the ground as he walked.

I saw his dark eyes, his strong, pugilistic build. Indeed he rolled on his feet a little as if he was still in the boxing ring of some fairground or boxing booth. His smile was smug and self-congratulatory. He did not see me, but turned from the drive and began to walk away from Riverside House.

A dreadful malaise assailed me. I felt again the blows he had rained upon my head and shoulders, heard his uncouth voice, knew that he had stood over me with his hands ready to press and prod and explore my defenseless body, though Mrs. Magwich had stayed him in his wish.

I smelled the malodorous floor again, heard the drip of dampness from the streaming walls, heard distant cries, smelled the stale and fetid smell of their establishment.

For the man who had visited Riverside House and was now leaving its environs was Robert Lessing.

I gathered myself together with an effort, and clung to the iron supports of the waterside steps. I felt the rough stones of the wall brush my hand. I stood still until I had gained control of my senses. I looked out over the river and, as always, the sight of the water calmed my mind.

Robert Lessing had clearly visited Riverside House to see someone, and that person was Evan, there could be no one else. It was now imperative that I go to see Evan, myself.

I continued up the steps and hastened to the house. There was a small study at the side of the house, attached to the conservatory, which was greatly used by Evan; it was there that he practiced with his dice, and read the French novels he affected to enjoy. I found him in the study;

he was sitting at the centre table, alone.

I saw that his face was ashen, and his hands were trembling. He looked at me as if he did not know me, as if he had never even heard of my existence. "You have had a visitor, Evan!" I cried.

"Indeed yes," he answered. "A man has been to see me, sent by another. A man from London who came to threaten me, and extort money from me, under pain of . . ." He stopped, unable to go on.

"I know this man!" I cried. "His name is Robert Lessing. He is responsible for the wounds upon my head and the bruises on my shoulders. It was he who attacked me, and is responsible for my losing my memory!"

Evan stared at me in amazement. "But how can this be possible?" he asked me. Then comprehension flooded his face. "So the house from which you escaped was the one which I myself visited! What a strange coincidence, Celeste. What extraordinary fortune has led out paths to cross!"

"Not entirely fortune," I answered. "There is some other explanation, I am sure of that, if we can only find it. But first, can you please tell me, Evan, of your predicament. Perhaps I may be able to help."

"I will tell you," he said, "since you know so much already and have been in this establishment. But as for helping me, please keep clear of this matter, Celeste. It is no concern for a woman. It is something I must solve alone.

"However," Evan paused, as if collecting his thoughts. "You will know of my proclivity, Celeste, that I am a gambler who loves his way of life, and seeks always to beat the odds at the tables, with cards, in cockfights, with dice, with God knows upon what matter the bucks of London fancy. But I assure you that this is my only vice. I have no other.

"On my last visit to London I tired of the Clubs of St. James's, and asked a coachman to take me to a floating game which would be unknown to me, where the odds might favour me. He took me to a house I did not know, in a street I had not frequented before. He assured me, when I paid his fare, that the establishment was well run, and that the games were not biased. He then laughed, and I wondered about it at the time.

"He had taken me to an establishment of a different purpose and nature, and one to which I was not accustomed. However, I did not know of the deception when I entered the foyer of this place. The proprietress introduced herself to me, and asked me my preference. I replied that I preferred chemin de fer, but that I would bet upon a fly's progress across a wall, if the company was convivial and the stakes attractive. She laughed, and informed me that she was actually running an establishment of a different nature, for in addition to the experienced prostitutes, she had several young girls who awaited despoliation. She offered to show me her wares, so that I could pick my victim. I felt overwhelmed with horror at this callous trade, and informed her I wished to have no part in it."

Evan paused. I had sat down facing him at the table. I saw again the dark passage which had led to my means of escape from Mrs. Magwich's house; I remembered how I had stood at the intersection of the two passages, and had observed Evan talking to the proprietress. I saw his expression, I heard his words.

"I am at a loss as to know how they traced me here," Evan continued. "I was in the entrance hall for a matter of minutes only, for as soon as I knew the truth of this house, I quit the premises instantly. Glad to escape. Appalled at the jape which had taken me there . . . Yet how they traced me here to Riverside House, I do not know."

"But you told them your name and address, Evan," I said. "I heard you distinctly. You identified yourself to

Mrs. Magwich. Perhaps this is the custom in a gaming house. I do not know. But you yourself told them. You delivered yourself into their hands."

"I do not recall," Evan said. "I had drunk a little it is true, or I would not have allowed this deception to take place. It must have been early in the conversation, when I still thought the house was a gaming house. I would not have told them if I had known the true nature of the place."

As if in a dream, I repeated to Evan. "I heard you say, I am Evan Terry of Riverside House, East Quayling . . . And don't you see Evan, that is where I first heard the words East Quayling! Clearly they stuck in my mind. And then, when I heard these words repeated by the young couple in the street market, in my confused state I decided that East Quayling must be my destination, that it held significance for me, must be the end of my search for refuge. In a strange way I followed you to East Quayling,

Evan! These words lodged in my mind and I obeyed their call."

"I only wish that you had followed me, truly, Celeste, with your memory intact and with resolution and intent! If only I were not halfway tied to Vinnie; if only this dreadful matter had not intervened to complicate things in my life!"

"What was the threat that Robert Lessing made, Evan?" I asked, for I did not wish to discuss this controversial subject, and I began to sense what that threat might have been.

"They naturally discovered that Lord Stanhope is my uncle, and that I am his heir. And they threaten me that . . . Unless I pay them a large sum of money, they will inform my uncle that I visited this bordello and what is more, took part in the practices there."

"But you did not stay!" I cried.

"Did you see me leave the premises, Celeste?" Evan asked me.

"Why no," I faltered. I closed my eyes, the better to fix the mental picture upon my mind. "I saw you standing there, talking to Mrs. Magwich. Heard your words. But . . . I cannot remember anymore."

"Yet I did leave," Evan affirmed stoutly. "Yet apparently it does not matter to Robert Lessing and Mrs. Magwich. The fact that I entered the premises and engaged them in conversation is, so they say, enough. Enough to inform my uncle of my presence there, enough to be a basis for their lies."

"You must not pay them, Evan," I cried. "This will be only the first of many extortions. Instead, you must go to your uncle and tell him the truth. Or to the authorities. Then this place can be raided and closed down!"

"Are you out of your mind, Celeste? Neither course is possible. I dare not approach my uncle with an account of this misadventure. He hates the gambling and drinking in London. And I know he seeks to put premises, such as Mrs. Magwich's, out of commission.

For me to admit that I had been there . . . " Sweat stood on his brow. His eyes widened. "Such action is unthinkable. It is out of the question and cannot even be discussed."

"At least go to the constabulary," I begged. "It would perhaps be possible to keep this matter from your uncle. At least they would end the trade of this dreadful establishment."

He shook his head. His eyes narrowed, and he looked at me reflectively. "You do not know the address of this place, do you, Celeste?"

I shook my head. I did not know where this house was situated. I had racked my brains and tortured my consciousness for clues which might give me the location of this place. But nothing came to mind. I did not know the address. But Evan did. And I must try to make Evan act.

"I do not know it but *you* know it, Evan. And for the sake of the young people kept prisoner there, you *must* go to official quarters, or to your uncle.

For their sakes, you must act."

I saw Evan screen his eyes from me. He turned his head away. "You do not know what you are asking, Celeste," he said. "My only expectations are from my uncle. I have no other income, no business in life. To inherit his money is my only hope.

"If I reveal the address of this place to either my uncle or the constabulary, my inheritance will be put in jeopardy. In the latter case, the confession would reach the ears of my uncle, never doubt. My whole life would be ruined, and my prospects brought to naught. No, I must keep quiet. Silence is my only protection."

I could not move him from this decision. In vain I pleaded. I even held his arm in my desire to persuade him to take steps to release Mrs. Magwich's victims. But he was adamant; he would not move.

"How will you raise the money to pay your blackmailers?" I finally asked.

"Not from my uncle, of course,"

Evan replied. "I have milked him too often, I dare not again. But I have some family heirlooms of gold which belonged to my father. A watch, a carriage clock, a fob, some gold chains. They will have to go. They should fetch a good price. I regret the necessity," he said stonily, as if nearing the end of his tether. "But at least I can buy time from Mrs. Magwich and Lessing. At least I can gain a respite so that I can consider what to do further."

I did not know it then, but these were the despairing words of many victims of extortion. Time could be bought, but at what a heavy price! And then time itself would be devoured by the dread of the next demand.

At this point I left Evan and went upstairs to my room. I felt a bitter disappointment that he would not reveal the address of Mrs. Magwich and Robert Lessing. I could only hope that involuntarily, of itself, this knowledge might return to my blank and troubled mind. But I did not think it likely, and this matter seemed to be without conclusion, and without hope.

Naturally, from this time my respect for Evan began to wane, and the attraction I had at first felt for him diminished of its own accord.

Later that day, Robin visited Imelda and assured her of his love, in spite of her condition. He assured her that her deep regret at not being able to give him a son, was her own regret, and hers alone.

He assured her that she was the one he wished to marry, whatever the state of her physical health. Time would solve the matter of his inheritors, he told her. No one can legislate for the future. If they could be joined in marriage and find their happiness and fulfillment in one another, that was all Robin asked, or expected of life.

Imelda came to see me, after this interview. "We have fixed the wedding for the autumn," she said. "And we both wish that you will be our bridesmaid, Celeste." I thanked Imelda for her kindness and preference, but begged not to commit myself to future events at this stage. It was as if I already knew that my own life might develop along unexpected lines, and that I might not be available for other concerns in the autumn.

Evan was delighted by the news, and Vinnie seemed pleased also. No doubt she thought that, with Imelda and Robin settled, her own romance with Evan might gather momentum and reach a happy conclusion.

For their affaire had recently hung fire; Evan had had other things on his mind, and Vinnie semed sometimes remote and rather strange in her attitude. In spite of my efforts to understand her, her personality remained an enigma, and her irascibility was often perplexing to everyone in her circle.

I was delighted, soon after these events, to receive a letter from Miles Stanley. I had ardently longed to receive such a communication. He had promised to write, but I knew that naval courses and exercises were arduous affairs which left little leisure. My heart almost stopped, when I received this mail.

I wish I could convey to you, dear Miss Celeste, the atmosphere and the rigours of this place. Modern weaponry is far outclassing the older type naval artillery, and there is much to be comprehended, and memorized.

The instructors and demonstrators are first class. I know Lord Nelson has commended them, himself, through my Lords of the Admiralty. But naturally they expect the highest standard possible, and their attitude is abrasive in the extreme to all gunnery officers, regardless of rank. It is like being a midshipman again, but without the lashes! Nevertheless all the weaponry officers take it in good part, and the teams try to excel. The *Victory* shall have the smartest gun teams in the whole of the navy! I am determined about that. Lord Nelson deserves no less. Villeneuve need fear us, I assure you. The French navy could well keep in harbour at Toulon rather than face our guns. Lord Nelson wishes for victory in every battle he undertakes. He need have no doubt but that his guns will uphold him when we face the enemy again.

I could not help but smile at the energy and enthusiasm so clearly expressed in this part of the letter. That Lord Nelson had a dedicated gunnery officer in Miles was clear. And that Miles must have Lord Nelson's confidence was apparent also. Indeed, the next section of the letter went on to reinforce this.

"I have written to Lord Nelson whilst on this course," Miles's brief went on, "and we have informed him of our progress and of the new developments which we can incorporate into the Victory's armoury."

His Lordship has replied to me in civil and indeed friendly terms, and he has asked me to visit him when I return home to East Quayling.

The invitation is for luncheon, and he has suggested that I should bring a guest.

I have therefore the honour to ask you, Miss Celeste, if you will accompany me upon this occasion. I feel sure you would enjoy it, and to meet Lord Nelson and Lady Hamilton in the flesh must be an inducement indeed to acceptance.

I am also writing to Miss Terry informing her of the invitation from Lord Nelson, and my suggestion that you should accompany me. I feel sure she will, as your hostess, grant you this facility. Please write to me and tell me your wishes in this matter! I assure you that I hope for your acceptance, and will do all on the occasion to bring you happiness and felicity.

The letter ended with the usual formal phrases. I laid down the pages.

An overwhelming sensation of happiness filled me, that I had heard from Miles. A letter would have been enough to fill me with delight, but to be asked to visit Merton exceeded all my dreams. I hastened to Imelda with my letter, but she was already reading her own epistle from Miles.

"But of course you must go, Celeste," she told me. "This is a signal honour indeed, to be received at Merton. Many local people angle for admittance, but are disappointed. Lady Hamilton and Lord Nelson receive guests from London, but they are naturally careful in their choice of acquaintances. They do not wish their privacy to be disturbed, and Lord Nelson, in spite of his naval conquests, is not always in the best of health.

"But with Miles at your side . . . you must have a new gown," Imelda added. "Do not protest. It will be a gift from myself, to celebrate my coming marriage to Robin, to repay you a little for your thought and kindness to me."

She was thoughtful for a moment, then said, "The call is for luncheon, so that means a day dress, yet formal and charming withal . . . " Imelda's voice ran on, as if she herself had been invited to Merton, as if she herself were the recipient of the sought after summons, as if her own heart was embellishing the coming occasion with enchantment and its own secret magic. A wild happiness filled me, and I held my hands to my face.

Yet not everyone was pleased by my good fortune. Vinnie appeared deeply disapproving.

I heard her talking to Imelda. "She came here out of the blue, and now she has everything. Miles Stanley's favour and now this invitation to Merton."

It was clear that Vinnie still hankered after Miles and felt rebuffed that she, a local young lady, had not been invited to Merton, while I, a stranger, had. I heard Imelda's voice speaking to Vinnie with reproof, but what the words were I could not hear, and indeed did not wish to distinguish. I still felt sorry for Vinnie, though her criticism of me did not make my feelings towards her easy.

However, I put all these reflections from me, and rejoiced in my letter from Miles and our coming excursion. And soon another shorter note arrived, which set out the date and the time of Lord Nelson's wish to receive us. I felt that my heart was near to bursting with pleasure and anticipation. My longing to see Miles again, and be in his company suffused the whole of my being and my life.

# 5

IT was upon a lovely summer's day that Judge Stanley's carriage arrived to take me to visit Merton. Miles descended from the conveyance, and helped me inside.

Imelda and Evan stood on the steps of the house to wave me farewell. The occasion was so momentous, the honour so immense to be received by Lord Nelson and Lady Hamilton, that I shook with nervousness, and Imelda and Evan tried to reassure me with their waving and cries of encouragement. The coachman cracked his whip, and the beautiful, well-cared vehicle of the Stanley family drew away.

Miles was also delighted to have sponsored the occasion. He began to talk to me about Lord Nelson at once.

"All his life he longed for an establishment ashore. As you will know, his marriage foundered, and he found his happiness with another family. Many people make the mistake of considering that Lord Nelson was primarily attracted to Lady Hamilton, when he decided to make his base within their home. But there was another factor involved, and one which is often ignored or discounted.

"Sir William Hamilton himself cared deeply for Lord Nelson. He respected and honoured him. He regarded it as a mark of favour that the Admiral should join his household.

"But as you will know, Sir William has been dead for two years now. And Lord Nelson and Lady Hamilton have spent but little time together. His lordship has been fighting at Cadiz, in the West Indies and in the Baltic Sea, so they have been separated. But now, at this time, there is a period of leave for the Admiral, and he is naturally spending it upon his property at Merton. A property he adores, and which is, of course, his very own."

I had heard say at Riverside House that Lord Nelson had bought Merton with his own money, descending into debt to do so. The Hamiltons then became his guests there. They were within *his* home, and not he in theirs.

I had heard also of Sir William's love for Emma Hamilton, a love which had never failed or faltered, until shortly before his death.

For the two lovers (for such they were, the world said) overstepped what Sir William regarded as the bounds of propriety, and offended him; his retaliation was swift.

Sir William saw his lawyers in London, and altered his will. Instead of leaving his wife as his heir, he bequeathed his possessions to James Greville, his nephew and the man with whom Emma Hamilton had lived previously.

Now, instead of having personal affluence, Lady Hamilton was finding that she was with very small personal resources. Lord Nelson, too, was pushed for money, and it was freely said that he owed money to the tradespeople in the district and roundabout.

Yet, they still entertained. Carriages drew up to the house and relatives and friends from London visited. Gossips openly asked how long this state of affairs could go on.

Naturally, I did not mention any of these reflections to Miles; they were hearsay only but, I was later to find, based upon truth. We chatted pleasantly of this and that, and Miles told me a little about the course in Portsmouth, and how he had acquitted himself under the examiners.

The River Wandle gleamed with its silver-blue colours as we took the riverside drive towards our destination. The sky was high, the clouds rounded and pearly white against the vivid blue. The lush foliage flanking the river waved a little in a tender breeze. I was glad that I had brought a parasol;

I thought the day ahead held nothing but promise of pleasure and felicity.

I was surprised when Merton came into our view. It was a pleasant square country house of red brick, with a formal garden. But beyond the main building were outhouses which clearly belonged to a farm. We could hear the cackle of geese, and ducks were wading on a small canal — a loop of the River Wandle — which ran close by the estate.

So Lord Nelson had bought himself a farm! And Lady Hamilton, I was to learn, excelled in managing the rural property. But all speculation was ended, as the carriage entered the approaches to the house. And I observed the figure of a man awaiting us in the garden.

To my surprise, I saw that Lord Nelson was of medium height, extremely thin, with rounded features and grey, almost white hair. He wore a black eyepatch upon his blinded eye. I do not know what I had expected, possibly a tall figure, commanding, with expansive gestures and a forthcoming manner. But Lord Nelson had none of these.

He was quiet in his movements and aspect, somewhat diffident on social occasions. He bowed before me, and took my hand, and I curtsied, myself overcome with the honour of the occasion. He welcomed Miles warmly, and held his arm with his free hand. It was then that I saw the empty sleeve, and remembered the cruel amputation at Tenderiffe which Lord Nelson had ignored, as he ignored the disability now. He indicated that we should first stroll in the garden, and set off before us, clearly anxious to show us his domain.

I saw now that the garden was set out on the same plan as the deck of a battle ship. "This is the poop," Lord Nelson said. "Here is the prow. See the gun turrets, Miles. Take care, Miss Celeste. We are approaching aft." We all laughed at these sallies, yet to Lord Nelson and also to Miles they had a touch of reality. It was as if they could not bear to be parted for too long from their honoured and trustworthy ship.

It was at that moment that I glimpsed what it would be like to be joined in marriage to a naval officer, to whom the sea and his service was the centre of his life. But I put such a thought from me sternly, for Miles and I were friends only, and no further advancement of our relationship had been mentioned or considered.

Lord Nelson suggested now that we should enter the house. I saw that Merton was built upon a square plan, with a central hall, and rooms opening off from the reception area. Pictures of Lord Nelson and depictions of his battles hung on the walls, and in the centre of the hall stood a replica of the foremast of that famous ship, *L'Orient*.

But all wonderment was put aside, as a lady entered the hall from the drawing room. And Lord Nelson presented Miles and myself to her. Lady Hamilton received us graciously, but in a somewhat abstracted manner, as if she had urgent matters on her mind, and, indeed, as if she had just remembered that we were guests for luncheon.

Lady Hamilton was of more ample build than I had expected, but she moved in an easy and fluid fashion, as if her increased girth did not affect her image of herself.

And indeed, she was passing beautiful, with thick dark hair, lustrous brown eyes, and small features in a well-shaped face. I could well understand how the painter Romney had fallen in love with her, and how she had been the toast of society in the prime of her younger days.

Clearly in Lord Nelson's eyes she was still the slim and elegant creature who had charmed him in Naples; she was still the talented centrepiece of many historical tableaux. Their attitude to one another was one of consideration and desire to please. They might have been young people in love, and not star-crossed lovers approaching middle age.

Lord Nelson now decided to take Miles to his study, no doubt to hear details of the weaponry course at first hand. Lady Hamilton took me into the drawing room, and there I was surprised to find quite a large gathering of guests assembled.

Wine was being taken, and the aroma told me that it was a vintage brand. A glass was pressed into my hand, and I began to make civil conversation with Mrs. Cadogan, Lady Hamilton's revered and capable mother.

Soon Admiral Nelson and Miles returned, and luncheon began. There were maids and servitors, and the food was plentiful and good. I noticed that the guests ate heartily, and drank the same; I began to see that the establishment was costly. Yet it was well run, and clearly gave Lord Nelson pleasure.

Lady Hamilton cut up his food into small pieces, so that he could manage to take his repast with one hand only. Her attitude to him now was that of a sister, solicitous and a little motherly. Later, I was to hear her flatter him outrageously; their relationship veered and varied in tone and accordingly to the occasion. Yet their rapture in one another was plain to see, and they clearly doted upon the child of the household, a little girl of five called Horatia.

The after lunch period sped swiftly by, and soon it was time to take our leave. I was not sorry to depart, for the noise of the household, the constant chatter, the rushing to and fro, the endless diversions had a perplexing effect on the mind and spirit. Perhaps Lord Nelson felt this also, for he seemed glad to escape with Miles and myself into the relative quietude of the garden.

We strolled for the last time along the simulated upper deck of the *Victory*; Lord Nelson's gaze was thoughtful as he strode the imaginary scene of his life's labours. Lady Hamilton suddenly appeared on the poop, alone. She joined the three of us, and in a few moments of calm fellowship, we strolled together.

At the gate of Merton there was a rosebush, and beside this tree Lord Nelson halted. He detached a single flower from its long thorny stem.

"It has been a pleasure to have made your acquaintance, Miss Celeste," Lord Nelson said to me. "Any friend of Miles Stanley would be welcome within my establishment, but you have made friends here on your own account, and we have found enjoyment in your company. Please accept this rose from Lady Hamilton and myself."

Lord Nelson paused thoughtfully before he handed the bloom over. "This could be called the Naples rose, the Copenhagen rose, a rose of the West Indies, a Santa Cruz rose." Still he halted, still he held the flower within his hand before he surrendered it to me. "But perhaps," he added, "it could be classified on an occasion to come. Perhaps the Trafalgar rose. Yes, that is it, Miles; I am sure I am correct. Please accept this, Miss Celeste, as the Trafalgar rose." And he finally placed the frail bloom within my hand.

"Come Horatio," said Lady Hamilton. "It is time for your rest." Her meaning was clear. Their hours together in privacy were approaching. She was civil, but she wished us gone. We obeyed the hint with alacrity, bowing to his lordship and her ladyship. Yet Lord Nelson stood still and watched us, as we entered Judge Stanley's carriage, and were driven away.

★ ★ ★

Miles asked me if I had enjoyed the occasion, and I assured him that I had indeed found pleasure in the luncheon and the illustrious company. We chatted easily, and then he seemed to pause in his discourse, and I guessed that he was considering a different matter upon which he wished to speak to me.

"Celeste," he began slowly, "the conditions of life in the navy and the hardships that these impose upon a service wife have lately been present in my mind. But . . . may I ask that you will consider them? There are the long separations inherent in service abroad, not always high pay. The strict discipline which somehow seems to reach into the home and touch one's wife. The traditions which can be restricting, the protocol which must be observed.

"But against this, is the high honour of serving one's county and fellow beings. Our oppositions to the French is imperative. One dare not think what would befall if the enemy should conquer our country, and impose a harsh and alien rule upon our women and children; we are obliged to fight the French and fight to win.

"There is also the camaraderie of the sea, and I am told that officers' wives share in this good spirit, and are ready to help each other endure the rigours of the service. There is the honour and glory of serving with a commander such as Admiral Nelson. And believe me, in the *Victory* there are the pick of England's fighting naval men. For myself, I found it a dignity beyond description to be one of their number. And I trust that my wife would share my feelings of honour, and would reinforce me in my desire to serve King George, and our fellow countrymen."

Miles fell silent, and we both watched the back of the coachman as he drove us along the banks of the Wandle, back to Riverside House and the end of our afternoon.

I felt at a loss for words. I did not know what to reply. That Miles was preparing me for a proposal seemed clear; yet our acquaintance was young and the problem of my nationality still hung over me. Indeed, I had been surprised that Lord Nelson had received me at all, since my country of origin was in such doubt. Moreover, the problem of my loss of memory was ever present.

I felt I must somehow lighten the occasion, also not wishing to take a false step at such a delicate moment. "I am sure you have mentioned this to many ladies before myself," I said. "Perhaps this dalliance is meant to please and amuse your partners upon social occasions."

Miles was not offended by these words, but seemed to understand my reply. "I assure you that this is no moment of dalliance," he said. "Also, I have never yet previously addressed any lady in these terms. I think you may have heard criticism of me — criticism of my behaviour, which was not understood.

"It is not that I have played with the affections of other young ladies, before we met, Celeste," he said. "Rather the truth of the matter is that, until now, I have been engaged upon a search — a search for a young woman to match the ideal within my mind. Not an ideal of icy perfection or superhuman attributes. But rather an ideal of being of compassion and beauty allied. In you, Celeste, I have met such a person; I have found the ideal that I sought, which I sometimes considered was forever out of reach."

He paused, and I said, "Please say no more at this juncture, Miles. There are many problems in my mind, and I must consider your statement, as you have wished me to do. We will meet again, I hope, and in the meantime . . . " I thanked him for the wonderful morning and afternoon, and my historic visit to Lord Nelson.

He bowed and kissed my palm, and I entered Riverside House with the Trafalgar rose in my hands.

★ ★ ★

Imelda came out of the drawing room, and took my hand and drew me into

123

the room, so that I could tell her all that had occurred. I told her of the warm reception we had received at Merton; and gave a description of the company and the household. However, I did not tell her of my final conversation with Miles. This was strictly private. In a strange way, I had still not entirely accepted it in my mind.

I went upstairs, and put the Trafalgar rose into a small vase on my dressing table. I began to remove my formal clothes, for I thought there must be some occasion upon which I could help Imelda. As I changed, I pondered the events of the day.

Love had shone from the faces of Lord Nelson and Lady Hamilton as they had waved us goodbye. Love had permeated the house and their lives. They had been criticized, I knew; Lord Nelson for his dismissal of Fanny, and Emma Hamilton for her partial abandonment of Sir William. Yet their love for one another had been the strongest emotion at Merton. It was as if they held themselves up to the judgement of the world, secure of final approbation because of the depth of their adoration for one another, and their long lasting commitment.

I walked to the window, and looked out at the River matters. I only knew that love was dominant in their lives. And love would hold them together, in spite of all the world could hurl against them, until their final parting.

As I put on my afternoon clothes, I could not help but feel a tender elation rush through me. Miles Stanley cared for me. I did not doubt but that, at a further meeting, he would make a formal proposal to me.

I walked to the window, and looked out at the River Wandle. What a strange quirk of fate had brought me here, to Riverside House, an unknown girl whose place of birth was still a mystery to her! Yet here I was, and this strange path in life had brought me to the man I loved. For yes,

I acknowledged my feelings; I loved Miles with a strong and steadfast love, and wished for nothing more or better in life than to become his wife.

It did not matter that the conditions of the service were harsh upon the female spouse; it did not matter that there were separations and hardship. I knew that all I wanted to do with my future was to be joined to Miles. I felt it was the happiest day of my life, when he had uttered the preambles to his proposal. I knew I would wait for his final declaration with a kind of secret rapture, and an anticipation that I knew would be more than fulfilled.

Imelda was in the conservatory when I went downstairs. "I assure you Celeste, there is no matter upon which I need your aid. Why not take a stroll along the towpath before tea? I myself am going to call upon the Vicar in East Quayling. I will not press you to come, for I feel you have done enough visiting for this day."

Imelda was in her outdoor clothes,

and I watched her quit the house upon her errand. I turned and went into the garden, and so I made my way towards the banks of the Wandle, a river which I had come to understand and love.

I walked further than I thought, for I had much to occupy my mind. So it was in the late afternoon that I turned my steps toward home. I traversed the pathway, enjoying the late day airs, the sheen of the water, the cry of the seabirds, the murmur of the reeds and rushes. It was not until I had reached the last lap of my homeward way, that I saw two figures standing athwart the entrance to the steps which led to Riverside House.

They were quite recognizable. My heart gave a lurch and I know that my lips parted in a cry. For waiting for me at the approaches to Riverside House were Mrs. Magwich and Robert Lessing.

# 6

"WE want to speak to you."

I saw that Mrs. Magwich was dressed in brown silk, with a bustle edged with lace and a shawl of velvet. Though her clothing was ornate, there hung about her a sense of disorder, a touch of incongruity and harshness.

Her body appeared still to be made of some solid substance, without the tender mould of flesh. Her soft and dough-like face was set in determined lines.

"That's right. We've been waitin' for you," Robert Lessing said. "You kept us waiting, but we got patience. Mrs. Magwich and I know how to bide our time."

"You see she is the right one, Robert. We thought it was she when we heard her description, and we were right," said Mrs. Magwich.

"What do you want?" I cried, and the words came through my clenched teeth. I began to tremble and for one dreadful moment, I thought I was going to collapse upon the towpath of the river.

"You've been interfering in our affairs," Mrs. Magwich said. "We've come to tell you that your unwarranted intrusion must cease."

"That's correct," said Robert Lessing. "You've been talking to Evan Terry and making him defiant. You've been working him up into opposition to our propositions. We can't have that. It is wrong to interfere in private matters between business associates."

"How dare you address me in these terms!" I cried. And suddenly, my whole attitude to the threatening pair before me changed.

Before they had frightened me. Their physical assault upon me and their designs upon my freedom and honour had horrified me, and filled me with fear. But now I felt instead of these emotions a searing anger, a calculated defiance, a wish to thwart them and to foil their plans. It was all I could do to stand still on the towpath and not approach them both and assault them, in their turn, with my clenched fists.

"Ho, she shows fight then," Robert Lessing said. "She is ready to oppose us. She is a fighting hen. Look, her face is red and her eyes flash. I like a capon with spirit. I like to see fight. It makes the surrender sweeter in the end."

"That is enough, Robert," said Mrs. Magwich. "Keep your desires for the proper occasions. This is important. This concerns money. She must be warned off, or she may undo all our intentions."

"You are in no position to extort money from Evan Terry," I told them. "He has committed no offense. He entered our house, it is true, but he did not stop to indulge in any of the practices you foster. He left almost instantly. As soon as he knew the nature of the place. What grounds are these for extortion? You have no ulterior hold upon him, and you know it."

"You are mistaken," Mrs. Magwich said. "It is not the guilty action itself which is the basis for extortion. It is the circumstances which surround the indiscretion, and the internal, private sensation of guilt which makes the victim pay out. Lord Stanhope, the celebrated reformer, is the key figure here," she said. "If he knew that his nephew had set one foot within the doorway of our establishment, do you for one moment believe that he would hold his nephew guiltless? Of course not.

"Evan Terry is as culpable in the eyes of the world as if he had been an habitué of our establishment. His protestations would be of no avail. For Robert Lessing and myself would testify otherwise. Nor need you try to find the coachman, for we have nobbled him. He has no memory of the occasion.

"There are also girls within our house who would swear that he had been partners with them in unnatural acts. You see, I have no illusion, no pride and no self-deception," Mrs. Magwich said, as she fixed me with her deep, black eyes. "We have Evan Terry in a vice, and you are powerless to help him."

"I will inform the magistrates," I cried.

"You will not do that," Mrs. Magwich replied. "You do not know our address. Also, you would not wish to plunge Miss Imelda Terry and her household into shame and confusion by bringing this to light. We have you too, you cannot move against us. Or it will be the worse for you, if you do that."

"That is a certainty," said Robert Lessing. "If you continue to interfere in our affairs, who knows, another accident might befall you."

"You escaped before," Mrs. Magwich

said, "thanks to Robert, here. But the next time there would be no escape. There would be no slip up. And the blow which befell you would be more serious. All our plans with you went awry through leniency, but there would be no leniency next time. There are many unexplained accidents these days, many of them fatal. Many never discovered. Play safe, and leave matters which do not concern you to those who know what they are doing."

I began to tremble. I know my colour heightened again. My whole frame shook with the violence of my emotion. "I will not forget your threats," I said. "I will not forget what you did to me and your record of vice. I will . . . "

"And what is there to prevent our informing a certain gentleman that you did indeed spend one night in the bordello?" Mrs. Magwich interrupted. "And Robert here initiated you into your womanhood? This would not go down well with a gentleman of high estate, such as you are friendly with now. Our words might be disbelieved. But the smear and doubt would remain. And all that is required in many cases is the half-doubt, the half-belief. These doubts can often sour a relationship more definitely than a direct accusation or proof of misdemeanour."

"You would not dare!" I cried vehemently.

"You do not know the extent of our daring," Mrs. Magwich said. "We must have dared greatly to have reached the pinnacle of affluence which we have now attained."

"I will see you are brought to justice somehow, if it is my last act on earth," I cried, almost beside myself with anger and opposition.

"Come Robert," Mrs. Magwich interposed. "She is ranting. No good ever comes of ranting, my dear," she said. "Emotions undermine the power of execution. Good day to you. Farewell. We shall meet again it is true, but on our terms, and not yours."

She turned to go.

"We have a carriage now," Robert said incongruously, and he waved his arm behind him.

I saw then, waiting on the road where it widened away from the village of East Quayling, a smart equipage with horses and a coachman upon the box.

The coachman had his head turned towards the three of us, clearly awaiting instructions from his employers.

"Remember," Mrs. Magwich said. "This has been no idle conversation, and these no idle threats. If you value your liberty, your future, and indeed your life you will stand aside from our concerns. Do not approach Evan Terry more. Leave him to his fate with us, or your fate may be considerably worse than his."

They turned then, and walked away along the towpath towards the carriage. Their progress was unhurried and strangely confident. It was as if three acquaintances had met and had held a brief conversation upon inconsequential matters, upon the river bank.

I saw them reach the carriage. The driver dismounted and opened the door. They entered their conveyance, and they did not look back; their purpose had been fulfilled. It was clear that they did not expect defiance or disobedience.

The two had tightened their nets upon their victims, and the occasions of inconvenience were over. They did not doubt that they held both Evan Terry and myself within the palms of their hands.

★ ★ ★

There was a grassy tussock near this strip of the river, and I went and sat down, resting my trembling limbs and aching head. For to see my two assailants again and hear their voices had brought about a return of pain and disturbance of vision. I rested for a few moments, trying to compose myself.

I realized that I must at once seek out a champion, and try to obtain advice as to what to do. For I was in no way going to lie down under the threats of this murderous pair. I was going to do something, something concrete and constructive to end their activities and bring them to their just deserts.

It was no use to return to Riverside House. No doubt Robert Lessing and Mrs. Magwich had already called there to see Evan, and had taken their cut from his possessions; there was no help there. He was only a victim in equal circumstances to myself.

I remembered that the house of Judge Stanley and Miles was not too far away. On an impulse I sprang to my feet, and turned my face towards Merton, for I knew that The Judge's House, as it was called, was situated not far from Lord Nelson's own dwelling.

I began to run along the towpath, hearing my breath on the air. I held my side with cramp, but I forced myself on. Soon I was obliged to walk, for the distance was much further than I had imagined. It seemed that miles stretched before me, along the edge of the River Wandle and I felt I could give up with fatigue and despair, but I pushed my weary limbs forward. At last I reached the detour within which The Judge's House was situated.

Miles had described his father's house to me, mentioning how it was set back from the River Wandle in a clearing of trees and lawns. The house was not large, but it was clearly in good order. It was said that Judge Stanley loved this house in the country, and came to stay here as often as he could quit his legal affairs in London.

I walked up the drive and rang the bell of the front door. This was opened by a middle-aged maid, who admitted me instantly. She bade me wait in the hall while she entered her master's study; within a few moments I was shown into this room.

Miles' surprise upon seeing me was

great and Judge Stanley was astonished also. Both men were taking a measure of wine together before dinner, chatting easily in the booklined study, with its leather covered chairs and desk. They rose to their feet, and Miles took my arms, and drew me into a deep and comfortable chaise. Before I could even speak, he pressed a glass of wine into my hand. I drank deeply at his behest, and the cordial immediately made me feel better.

"This is clearly no trivial matter on which you have come, Celeste," Miles said. "But before you speak, may I present my father." And Judge Stanley stood before me, bowed, and took my hand into his own.

I saw that Miles's father was a tall man of broad build, and commanding presence. His skin was light in colour, his cheeks ruddy, as if he loved the open air. His hair, now thinning, was light brown and worn *en brosse*.

He wore the informal clothes of a countryman, as Miles had previously worn the clothing of a crewman. His eyes were direct in their regard — searching, but not unfeeling or aggressive. I gained the impression of a man who was scrupulously fair, but inclined to mercy. This was an attribute of many of the judiciary at this time.

But he was speaking to me in kindly tones. "So this is Miss Celeste, the house guest of Miss Terry at Riverside House. Welcome to The Judge's House! Our hospitality is yours. I beg you to tell us what we may do for you."

Without preamble I began to speak. I did not worry that my hair had fallen from its combs, that my shoes were dusty, my dress crumpled from my long run along the towpath. I only knew that I must tell Miles and Judge Stanley what had occurred. If they could do nothing to help, at least I needed their careful attention.

I told the two men everything. Miles knew much of my previous history, and of how I arrived at Riverside House. But of course the recent conversation with Mrs. Magwich and Robert was new to him. Judge Stanley listened with great attention and an air of purpose and reserve.

"These two malefactors are well known to the civil authorities," Judge Stanley said at the end of my recital. "The constabulary have been trying to find their premises for years, without result. Have you any clue, any small feature which might aid the search?" I shook my head. I had pondered this for so long and I was certain I had nothing new to reveal or add.

"They also change their premises from time to time," Judge Stanley said. "They did not tell you this, but it is the case. They are known for the crimes of violence and extortion. I know the London runners would regard it as a triumph to get their hands on this pair."

"You say they had a carriage, Celeste?" Miles asked me. "Surely, if I took our own carriage and hastened after them I might overtake them?"

Miles added to his father.

"The time is too far advanced," Judge Stanley replied. "They have clearly outdistanced you now. And they are not so stupid. They are not likely to approach their premises by any direct route, but will use byroads until they reach London."

"Could we not see Evan Terry?" Miles asked his father. "Evan knows the address. He has only to divulge it, to bring the matter to a close."

"I advise you not to approach Evan," his father returned. "Pressure at this point might prove disastrous. I have known victims of extortion to do tremendous harm to themselves when challenged by their family or friends. After all, all their efforts are directed towards keeping their frailties from their associates. To show them that their efforts have been in vain often proves too much for their sensibilities. Please do not approach Evan, Miles. And Miss Celeste, I beg you not to mention this matter to Evan in any form."

Reluctantly, I agreed. In my present forthright frame of mind I wished that the three of us might confront Evan, and somehow force him to reveal the address. Yet a calmer state would reveal the correctness of the Judge's advice. I looked at the Judge with new respect, and listened as he spoke.

"I will mention this matter in London and make further enquiries there. My offices are in Poutney Lane, near to the Law Courts. If you should ever need me, when I am in London, you will find me there. I am certain that we can solve this matter without adding to Evan's distress. Leave the problem with me. I will do all that I can to solve this dilemma for you all."

"And now, Miss Celeste," said Judge Stanley. "I insist that you stay and partake of the evening meal with us. Miles! Please tell Maud. And instruct Laxton to ride over to Riverside House to inform Miss Terry as to where Miss Celeste is being entertained. No! I insist. And Maud will take you upstairs to a guestroom where you can compose yourself, and prepare yourself to partake of dinner with Miles and myself."

I had no option save to do as I was bid. I welcomed the quietude of the guestroom where I could comb my unruly hair, and wash my flushed face. I straightened my dress also, as my racing along the river pathway had undone the belt of my bodice and the neck fichu was all awry. I felt that I presented quite a different picture to my two hosts when I went downstairs and entered the dining room.

I would like to record the great pleasure this meal with Miles and his father gave to me. I saw that, in spite of the lack of a woman in their lives (for Miles' mother was long since dead), they coped exceedingly well, and were efficiently served by Maud and her staff.

The conversation was gay and lively, yet I sensed beneath it an undertone of seriousness. I realized that soon Miles must depart upon his service with Lord Nelson in the *Victory*, and that Judge Stanley must return to London, and leave the place he clearly loved so well.

Therefore, at the end of the meal I begged to be excused and prepared to make my departure. In spite of my protests, Miles insisted on accompanying me in the carriage back to Riverside House. I protested, in vain for I guessed that these closing hours of kinship were deeply valuable for both father and son. Yet they would have none of it, and with Miles by my side, Laxton drove us over in the Judge's carriage to the Terry household.

★ ★ ★

Although it was now late in the evening, I was surprised to find both Imelda and Evan talking together in the hall.

"Evan I'm *very* concerned. Three of the antique snuffboxes are missing from the display cabinet," Imelda told him.

"And the candlesticks from the library . . . Evan, they are of solid silver with gilt trim!"

There was no response from Evan and she continued: "Evan . . . it's so distressing — too awful to think of even — that any of the staff are thieves. But what other explanation is there?"

Evan was at the foot of the stairs. He mumbled some answer to his sister, and then hastily mounted the treads.

We both watched him go. I did not doubt but that these precious items mentioned by Imelda had been handed over to Mrs. Magwich and Robert. It was clear that having taken all his money, they were now engaged upon milking him of the choicer items of Riverside House.

"And who were your guests, Evan?" Imelda called after Evan's retreating figure. "I am told by Janet that you received this afternoon, but I do not know the identity of the callers."

Imelda turned to me. Her face was both angry and troubled. It was plain she was both puzzled and perturbed by recent events.

It was now upon the tip of my tongue to tell Imelda the truth, that Evan was being blackmailed, and that the family heirlooms were being filched from them as a pledge of silence. But I remembered Judge Stanley's words. Also, I was suddenly reluctant to add to Imelda's distress by the revelation of her brother's escapade. I realized strongly that it was up to Evan to clear himself by his own confession to his sister. Not by means of a telltale or other accusing person.

After a short conversation with Imelda, I went upstairs to my room. I felt deathly tired, yet I had much to think about.

First there was my unflinching determination to oppose Mrs. Magwich and Robert Lessing with all the strength and energy of which I was capable.

I found I did not care about their threats to me. Before I had feared them, but now . . . Now I was determined to do all I could to bring them to justice, and to end their reign of terror to the victims of their immoral trade.

I felt I had a strong ally in Judge Stanley. There was no doubt he had extensive contacts in London, not only among the judiciary, but with the police. But I was determined not to rely upon the Judge alone. I decided to keep watch in the future, to observe events closely, and then to make what plans I could for the downfall of this evil pair.

I undressed and slipped into bed. I could hear the River Wandle, moving sweetly along its course. I lay and calmly reflected upon my own mental state.

The sight of Mrs. Magwich and Robert waiting for me on the towpath had jolted my mind. It was as if a box containing a jigsaw had been shaken, and the pieces rearranged.

Images floated before my inner eyes. Again the sea, the quay, ancient buildings, placid home life, and suddenly, a square house within a square garden, behind a square wall. Then the images faded and I fell asleep.

I awoke in the night, and happiness flooded through me. Though I had been perplexed by events, yet my own affairs now brought me nothing but delight.

I remembered Miles' conversation with me on the way back from Merton; how he had prepared me for the conditions of a naval officer's wife. I had been convinced then that he was near to a declaration.

And then again, on the drive home from The Judge's House to Riverside House, Miles had addressed me with tenderness, assuring me of his regard, approaching the moment when he would ask me to be his wife. That moment was still to come; that occasion of bliss was on the close horizon. But I lived the heavenly moment in anticipation. I felt that life had no greater bliss to offer me than what was to come.

I crushed from my recollection the problems of my nationality and my loss of memory, and the appalling question of Evan, Mrs. Magwich and Robert Lessing. Surely a benign Fate would help to solve these difficulties for me?

The main thing was that I had traveled to Riverside House in my forgetfulness, and had met the man I loved, and that our relationship was approaching completion.

And so I fell asleep. The River Wandle flowed swiftly by, but not more swiftly than unknown events were moving towards me.

For upon the following day incidents would occur which would amaze and astound me. The memory of this day affects me still. I had no premonition, no warning. Events occurred as a flash of light from the sky like a meteorite falling to earth.

And I was not the only one to be deeply affected by these happenings and their culmination.

# Part Two

Part Two

# 7

THE day began in ordinary fashion. I knew that no immediate meetings had been planned between myself and Miles, as Miles was leaving East Quayling early that morning to attend the admiralty in London and that Judge Stanley was also to quit his country retreat for a furlough upon the bench in the Law Courts.

When Imelda came downstairs, I sensed that she was feeling unwell, and was in a troubled state of mind. It was as if she knew her brother was in dire difficulties. But she could not fathom what these were, or from where the threat to him emanated.

I tried to cheer her, with various topics of conversation which I thought would please her, but she would not respond. Even a discussion of the immediate arrangements for her forthcoming marriage to Robin Marchmant failed to divert or interest her.

Robin rode over to see his fiancée during the morning, and was greatly concerned by her depressed condition. "Please all come to dinner this evening at Claremont Hall," he said. But Imelda refused the invitation, and was unmoved by Robin's attempts to cheer her. "Well, allow us to come to Riverside House this evening, and partake of the evening meal with yourselves," Robin continued. "I will bring some newly bought wine, and I know that Celeste will attend the menu."

I instantly agreed, and Imelda accepted the arrangement, with some small show of animation. I left Robin and Imelda together to talk of their private affairs while I went to the kitchen.

I prepared a charlotte russe, of which Imelda was very fond, and also a comfit of fruit with fromety. Janet entered into the spirit of the occasion and roasted and basted carvings of lamb and veal. I prepared duchesse potatoes, which were a novelty in England at this time. I began to hope that the coming evening dinner might help Imelda to regain her good spirits, since I naturally felt great sympathy with her in her mood of depression. Only I, apart from Evan, knew from whence it sprang.

Evan remained in the study all day. He looked ill and strained. Though I remained vexed with him because he would not go to the police and end the reign of terror of Mrs. Magwich and Robert, not only for himself but for others, I felt sympathy with him too. So often are we torn apart when our emotions conflict, and human suffering affects us even when we disapprove in our hearts.

Robin and Vinnie drove over from Claremont Hall at around six o'clock, and Robin busied himself decanting the wine. A little while later, the two families sat together in the drawing room, sipping a measure of the new

155

dry sack, and informing Robin of our opinions. Imelda had cheered up a little by this time, and it was clear that the efforts of Robin and myself had done much to bring colour back into her cheeks, and the old brightness to her eyes.

It was approaching the time of the serving of the meal when I looked out of the drawing room window and saw a carriage drawn by two horses coming along the drive.

The carriage halted outside the front door, and the whole assembly in the drawing room now gave this new arrival their attention, for the equipage was unusual in the extreme.

This was clearly a carriage of an official organization; a carriage used by high ranking military or naval men, or even by the police. Two footmen sat on the box, and the horses were groomed and beribboned. The coach itself bore a coat of arms, but this was not familiar to any of us.

We saw a coachman alight, open the

door of the carriage, and a man stepped down. He walked without preamble, with long strides and an air of authority to the front door.

We heard Janet answer the knock, and then heard voices. Janet appeared in the doorway. "There is a gentleman to see you Miss," she said. "A foreign gentleman. I cannot understand his name."

"Please show this gentleman in," answered Imelda, who was as mystified as any of us. It was as if she thought she might require our support, instead of seeing the strange visitor alone.

"Allow me to present myself, Madame," said a deep yet melodious voice. "I am Captain Ralph van de Meuve of the Belgian navy." And the gentleman in question stepped into the drawing room and bowed to the assembled company.

We all stared at the newcomer with surprise, for indeed he would have made a sensation in any gathering.

He was tall, broad shouldered, with

fair hair to the colour of gold curling tightly around his head. His features were a little bold, his colour high and fresh. He had a mobile mouth that could show command when he smiled at us; we saw that his teeth were white and even.

The Captain had addressed himself to Imelda, seeming with one glance around the room, to signal out the chatelaine of the house. "Please allow me to present my credentials to you, from the Belgian Embassy," he said. And Captain van de Meuve approached Imelda and placed a letter within her hands.

The Captain stood still, awaiting Imelda's scrutiny of the documents, yet his stillness was of no passive nature; he was motionless, but it was as if his body was still engaged in direct and purposeful action.

He surveyed each of us in turn. His eyes rested upon myself, and he smiled. He seemed to cast a spell around him of control encompassing us all. A strange dynamism flowed from him. He was the most potent and authoritive human being I had ever encountered.

"I accept your introduction, Captain," said Imelda shortly. "But may I ask your errand in this household, and how we may assist you?"

"I have come to see Miss Celestine Cunningham," the Captain said. "Who is a guest in your house, and has been for some time."

"And what is your errand, pray, with my guest?" asked Imelda, masking her surprise at hearing this unaccustomed name, a surprise shared by everyone in the room, including myself.

For answer the Captain crossed the room and stood before me. Again he smiled, his frank, open, yet commanding smile. He took my hand in his.

"Celestine. Don't you know me?" he said. "It is I, Ralph.

"I am your fiancé, and I have come to take you home."

Incongruously, at these words, I noticed that Ralph van de Meuve's uniform was of dark blue, heavily frogged with gold braid.

I raised my eyes to his face; I felt almost mesmerized by the intent gaze of his eyes. But so far as I knew, he was a stranger to me. He was a man I had never seen before.

Imelda was speaking. "Captain, you have astonished us by your arrival and statement. But it is up to Celeste to acknowledge you. Until then . . . " She shrugged her shoulders. "You are a guest here. May I ask you to be seated and to accept a glass of wine."

"Do you not believe my words, Madame?" asked Ralph van de Meuve, still standing.

"I accept your credentials from the Belgian Embassy, and I believe that you are who you represent yourself to be. But as for being the affianced of Celeste . . . That is another matter entirely.

And one which must be investigated and proved."

It was at this moment that Janet came to the door and announced that dinner was served in the dining room. Imelda could do no other than ask the Belgian Captain to be her guest. But I thought she did this cooly, and with a lack of enthusiasm. The Captain accepted the invitation, and after sending a message to his coachman to accommodate themselves in the kitchen, accompanied us into the dining room, where the viands were already sliced and laid out for serving.

It was a strange, strained meal. There was a definite sense of opposition to the Captain. Perhaps this was due to the surprise of his arrival and the unexpected nature of his statement. I felt the eyes of the family upon myself and the Captain. I ate little, since all zest for the meal which I had so lovingly prepared had left me.

"Come and sit beside me, Celeste,"

said Imelda when we had assembled in the drawing room. It was as if she wished to give me support. "Captain van de Meuve, we await your explanations. We imagine that you have some elucidation of this matter ready, and we will hear you out."

Ralph sat beside Robin. He appeared to marshal his thoughts, and then began.

"You will see from my credentials that I am a liaison officer between the Belgian and the British navies. For this purpose I spend some considerable time in England, and travel between the two countries as required. My home is in Bruges, and my family is an ancient one, and is well thought of in Belgium and that city.

"As for Celestine here," the Captain said, and he turned his head and regarded me, his gaze kindly and tender, "she also lived in Bruges. She was brought up there, and that city is her home. Celestine is the daughter of an old sea captain, Adam Cunningham, who sailed out of Bruges for many years. After his death, she made her home with her aunt, Madame la Foche, and her companion, Miss Preston, who was once Celestine's governess. I tell you this," the Captain continued, "because I know what has happened to Celestine, and that she has lost her memory. I am hoping that this recounting of events will help to restore her recollection, and recall to her her former life — and her present position in my life," he added.

"Please resume, sir," said Imelda, and Robin agreed. As for myself, I felt hypnotized by this man and his strange discourse.

"Celestine and I had been acquainted from our earliest years," Captain van de Meuve resumed, "and it was in the natural course of events that we should fall in love and become engaged. There is some difference in our ages," he admitted, "but I felt that my greater years would help me to care for her, and to give her the security her father would have wished for her."

At these words, a stirring of opposition awoke in me, I felt that I was being discussed as a package, and that, indeed, was how the Captain saw me. As something to be preserved and wrapped up! But I did not see myself as a precious object, and I knew that life — indeed I had learned the hard way — has its difficulties and terrors for us all. And no one can fully protect another person from its battles and internal strifes.

Imelda was quick to seize upon this point. "Celeste has revealed herself to us as a competent person, and one well able to run her own life," she said. "But I honour your intentions, sir," she added, trying to be fair. "Please resume, that we may judge this matter further."

"Although Celestine and I had not set the date of our wedding, it was deemed fitting that Celestine should travel to London, while I was myself in the capital, and there she would choose her wedding gown.

"She was accompanied by Miss Preston, who had by this time become companion to Madame la Foche, and was an honoured and respected member of the household.

"The two ladies landed at Tilbury, and it was in the environs of the docks that disaster struck at them. Two ruffians, a woman and a man, attacked Miss Preston, beating her to the ground, and rendering her unconscious. They struck also at Celestine, but with not so much force. They had a conveyance nearby, and into this they lifted Celestine and abducted her to their premises. I am told that this was a favourite ploy of this notorious pair. To meet a foreign vessel at the docks, and there to perform their work of assault and kidnap. They deemed a foreign girl particularly vulnerable, since the language difficulty rendered her all the more defenseless.

"The matter was over in a matter of minutes, and in the melee around the docks, the whole event went unobserved by disembarking passengers. It was not until some hours after the event, that Miss Preston was found in an insensible condition in an alleyway close to the dockyards.

"The Bow Street runners were fetched, and she was removed to hospital. In her handbag, the constables found a record of my name and my address at the Belgian Embassy. They communicated with me at once. Naturally, I was deeply concerned over this matter, and particularly over the disappearance of Celestine. Miss Preston could aid neither the police nor myself by any description of the assailants. The attack had been swift, and had been affected upon unsuspecting persons from the rear."

At this point Captain van de Meuve fell silent, and I thought that the atmosphere of the room had thawed a little towards him. I was still surprised at the coolness with which his recital was being received; I saw both doubt and hesitation expressed upon the faces of Robin and Imelda. Evan sat silent, pale as a ghost, hearing of the exploits of his tormentors. Only Vinnie seemed to have a friendly spirit towards the foreign Captain. She rose to her feet and advanced toward him.

"Please allow me sir, to offer you a glass of port. Robin, should not the entire company partake of a little extra refreshment?" She crossed to the sideboard and held towards her brother a decanter he had earlier filled. The Captain appeared refreshed by the wine, and soon resumed his discourse.

"I am told that it has proved difficult to trace the whereabouts of Celestine's attackers. The police have been searching for them for some time. Yet by some skilfull means they keep out of the reach of the law. Would that I myself could find them," he added. "I would with my own hands serve out to them what they delivered to Miss Preston and Celestine."

I did not glance at Evan, but I

know he shifted uneasily. The truth was getting very near to home now, I thought. I did not know how he could live with his conscience and keep silence when he knew so much, but his pale face was shuttered as a trap. He valued his inheritance more than truth, justice — or, it seemed, another person's life.

Captain van de Meuve had taken the chair next to mine, and he now gently took my hand and held it in his own.

"You traveled to East Quayling, did you not, Celestine, in a cart owned by a young couple who work a small farm beyond East Quayling? This young couple were concerned for you, but, because of illness, did not travel to London market with their wares for some time. When they finally came again to the capital, they thought it their duty to be in touch with the authorities. They told the magistrates at Bow Street of the young girl who had received a blow to the head, and who had fled from London in fear and distress. They described how they had left their passenger on the riverside approaching East Quayling. They had not seen or heard of her again.

"The officers in charge thought, from the description, that it was possible that the young lady who had traveled to East Quayling, might be the same young lady who had been assaulted at the docks. They wondered how she had escaped. With commendable thoroughness, the officers considered that enquiries might be worthwhile, so that the identity of the lady might be established.

"I offered to help, since I was directly interested in the case, and also, I held some official position in London, which influenced the police to allow me to carry out my own investigation. And so I traveled to East Quayling, and made my own enquires there. I soon heard, when I visited the inn called The Hero, of the foreign young lady who was a guest at Riverside

House. Her description tallied with yours, Celestine, and so . . . Here I am, dear Celestine. I have traced you at last, and I am overjoyed that at last we can be reunited."

At those final words the Captain raised my hand to his lips, and kissed my wrist and hand. But I felt no pleasure in the salute. I was at a loss, bewildered and deeply perplexed by the whole situation.

"And what now are your plans, Captain, may I ask?" Imelda was saying. "What is your immediate course, now you have found Celeste?"

"I have come to take Celestine back to her rightful home," Ralph van de Meuve said. "Celestine, I have come to take you back to Bruges."

★ ★ ★

At these words there was consternation in the room. No word was said; no one moved. And yet, a kind of silent reaction gripped everyone

170

present. Imelda was the first to speak. "Of course sir, such a course could not be agreed upon." Her voice was icy in the extreme, and her eyes, usually so warm and full of good humour, were cold and distant. Her attitude was almost unfriendly.

"And why not, madame, may I ask?" enquired Captain van de Meuve.

"Celeste is a guest in my household. She has become as almost a member of our family. I could not for one moment agree to her leaving Riverside House, unaccompanied, with a gentleman whose acquaintance we have only recently made."

"Are you implying, madame, that I may not be a fit person to be escort to Celestine?"

"By no means," Imelda replied. "But the conventions must be respected. Celeste does not leave this house without further investigation. And a chaperone."

"I could supply a chaperone, madame, who would meet with your approval,"

Ralph said. Then he added, "May I suggest that we ask Celestine herself what her reactions are to my proposals?"

I glanced at Ralph as he spoke, and saw that his expression showed both kindliness and concern. I shook my head

"I am quite unable to add anything to this discussion," I answered. "I respect Captain van de Meuve, but have no wish to travel overseas in his company."

"There you are," said Imelda, with a kind of triumph. "Also, I could not dream of allowing Celeste to leave my home in the present state of her memory."

Ralph van de Meuve was clearly put out, and surprised at this opposition. "I am fully aware of Celestine's lack of memory," he said. "But there are eminent doctors in Bruges who could attend her. I understand that, after the first examination by the local doctor, no further medical attention has been given her. I intend, now I have resumed my position as her fiancé, to remedy that."

It was true that I had had no medicaments for my loss of memory, beyond Doctor Hedges' first attentions. But I myself had trusted to nature to restore the balance of my mind. I felt we had all done the right thing and dreaded to be probed or examined by medical men who might force the pace too rapidly for my returning recollection.

My memory was returning, bit by bit, I was sure of that. Even now at this moment I felt that some advancement was about to be made. I waited, but no images came. I heard Imelda say:

"It has been our pleasure to have had you as a guest for dinner, Captain. But I regret we cannot offer you hospitality at Riverside House."

I looked at Imelda with surprise, for there were several guest rooms at the big house, all of them ready for occupation, thanks to my own efforts in rearranging and refurbishing.

"Perhaps we could offer the Captain

hospitality at Claremont Hall?" Vinnie asked Robin.

"You forget that the guest rooms are under reconstruction," Robin replied. And I saw a glint in his eyes that indicated that he did not intend to permit the Captain to stay in his house.

I was surprised at the resurgence of hostility. Within his own lights, I thought, Ralph van de Meuve had done nothing wrong or out of place.

But he was replying to Robin and Imelda: "I thank you for your acceptance of myself at the evening meal, and in your drawing room. But I am already lodged at the Hero Inn, and my entourage with me.

"I will withdraw with your permission, and trust I may be given leave to return tomorrow."

The Captain turned towards me, and again took my hand in his. "Goodnight Celestine. We will talk again on the morrow. And I am certain I can aid your memory. Trust me, please. We have much to discuss, and much to resolve. And I am not one to be disconcerted, or easily put off my legal and personal course."

★ ★ ★

I felt that I did not really wish to have any further discussions over the Captain's visit, and I asked to be excused, to make my way upstairs.

To my surprise, Vinnie accompanied me. "Can I aid you, Celeste? I will bring you a warm drink when you are settled.

"What you have gone through! I did not realize the difficulties of your course! But now the Captain has arrived, much will be made clear, and much solved."

She fussed over me a little when I reached my bedroom. I wondered if her changed attitude was because she thought I would no longer be a contender for Evan, and that Miles would now be beyond my bounds.

175

I slipped into bed, and lay still. As I expected, the coming of the Captain had acted as a catalyst, and images in my mind began to unfurl.

I saw the city of Bruges before me. The ancient cathedral, the medieval buildings, the canals, the street markets, the tiny, cultivated gardens.

I saw the house which had been my home. It was called the Harbour House, and was almost on the docks itself. From the windows one could see the eternal panorama of shipping, the skies, the gulls, the masts, the lanterns, the intricate riggings. I could hear the sounds of the harbour, the city, and my home.

Voices. I could hear voices. Women's voices. Cries of seafarers, cries of stallholders and shopkeepers, cries of children, bells of the churches and cathedral. All the sounds of the ancient city rang around within my head.

But I could not remember people. I could not remember my aunt, Madame La Foche, or Miss Preston, the governess turned companion, with whom I had traveled to London.

I could not remember my father, now dead, nor my mother who had predeceased him. And I could not remember Ralph, or the occasion of my engagement. I could only remember in connection with Ralph, a square house, in a square plot of land, and square furniture, dark, polished, and old.

* * *

During the night I awoke. It was as if a tide was sweeping through my head, as if waves were battering against a stout wall or strong rocks.

I still could not see faces or figures, but emotions strong as steel enveloped me.

There had been opposition to my engagement to Ralph. There had been doubt; there had been the overriding of doubt. There had been hesitation, a desire not to offend, and sweeping away of scruples.

There had been dominance, a need for certainty, a desire to know love. There had been longing, unfulfilled, a question still pursued and not yet achieved with finality. There had been a trusting that had turned to ashes.

I awoke. My nightshift was sopping wet with perspiration, and I was trembling and shaken. I heard my voice crying out, but I stifled my utterances. This was a climacteric I must bear alone. Undoubtedly these traumas were my memory trying to reassert itself. I must be passive and wait, as if for a visitation.

And in the morning when I awoke, I knew that I was changed — and that I welcomed the change. For the alteration in myself had made my way ahead quite clear.

# 8

IN the morning, Imelda said, "Captain van de Meuve has given me the address of your aunt, Celeste, and I am going to write to her today. If the response is favourable, I will myself accompany you to Bruges. I feel that this is both my duty and my right. You should not travel into another country unless I am by your side."

I knew also that Imelda wished to see Madame La Foche, and satisfy herself as to her status and character. I felt rather amused by this, but attempted not to let Imelda see my reaction.

"You may have difficulty in getting to Bruges, sister," said Evan to Imelda. "I am told they are clearing the seas, preparatory to Britain's offensive against the French. Even the mail has difficulty in getting through, now. I am informed that the last visitors have been allowed in. England is going to be almost under siege during the coming battle with France. Your hopes of reaching Bruges are very slim indeed, Imelda."

Imelda ignored this. "Captain van de Meuve has sent round to ask if he might visit us at eleven o'clock this morning," she said. "I trust this will be convenient for you, Celeste? I suggest that you receive the Captain in the conservatory, where it is cool and private. No doubt you will both have a great deal to talk about."

Punctually at eleven o'clock Ralph presented himself at Riverside House. I looked with interest as he entered the conservatory. It was as if I was observing him for the first time.

His figure was so tall, so compelling in aspect; his uniform, although unfamiliar to English eyes, added to his air of command and authority.

He smiled and his blue eyes, so clear, so vivid in colour lit up with the cordiality of his emotions. He took my hand courteously and raised it to his lips. I saw the tight curls of his golden hair as he bent his head over my palm. He sat beside me on a garden chaise, and his attitude was sympathetic and attentive. He waited, as if to give me opportunity to speak.

I was silent. Ralph was clearly going to force no pace of intimacy; he had established himself as my fiancé, but beyond that he was not going to trespass into any of the familiarities which his status might grant him.

Until I myself gave the word. I suddenly deeply respected him for this, and knew that this was no ordinary man, but one of sensitivity and discernment. Yet the driving force within him bade him speak to me, when I did not address him. I listened attentively to his words.

He spoke in general terms about my school, my governess, the church we attended. He mentioned mutual acquaintances and friends of the family.

I made some responses to these subjects, and found them deeply interesting, but I could not put a face or form to the names he uttered. This part of my life continued to remain a complete blank to me.

He spoke of his mother, Madame van de Meuve, and the family fortunes. I was attentive, but no spark of animation lightened my mind.

I thought that Ralph was disappointed by my reactions. Imelda entered the conservatory after about half an hour, and offered us refreshment, but we both declined the offer and Ralph rose to leave.

"I am obliged to quit East Quayling for a few days. I have been recalled to my embassy for other duties," he told us. "You will know that the whole of your navy is being prepared for the battle ahead. Belgium is, of course, neutral in this conflict. But naturally there are legal and other matters we must discuss with the British.

"I have English naval personnel to

see, and various details of protocol to arrange. I beg you to excuse me for a matter of days, Celestine. I will be in touch with you immediately upon my return."

"Do you intend then, to spend much time in East Quayling, Ralph?" I asked my visitor.

"But of course, Celestine. The whole aim and object of my private life now, is to aid you to recover your memory.

"Naturally, I hope soon to resume our former relationship. We have much to discuss concerning the future. Our marriage, and our future home."

We walked out into the garden from the conservatory. Suddenly, I said to Ralph, "There is a square house sometimes, in my thoughts. Within a square garden, and furnished in a rectangular way."

Pleasure shone upon Ralph's face. "So you have remembered!" he cried. "The house of which you speak is called La Jola! It was prepared for us as our future home!

"My mother owns the property, and she herself furnished it for us. Celestine, I am so gratified! This is the first indication of your returning recollection. I pray God that this trend will continue, and that we shall soon be on our old footing, and with our married life to look forward to."

I watched Ralph go. How handsome, he was, I thought. How manly. How competent to face every eventuality of life. He had spoken modestly of the family finances, which I guessed were considerable. He was an ideal fiancé for any girl or woman. What more could anyone ask of life save this dynamic and successful man? But I felt only sadness as I watched him walk away.

★ ★ ★

It was as if Imelda and the rest of the family knew that I had long thoughts to think; and many aspects of my life to consider. They did not approach me during the morning, but allowed me the privacy my deliberations needed.

Soon I went to walk beside the Wandle, knowing that the sights and sounds of the river would aid me in my reflections. I watched the seabirds, and trailed the river grasses in my hands. The sweet smell of the water and the distant cries of the village fisherman soothed me. I had much to face, and I determined to confront my dilemma squarely.

There was no doubt but that I had become engaged to Ralph in my immaturity, and that he had swept me off my feet.

He was considerably older than myself; he had himself told me that he was in his early thirties. He must clearly have overwhelmed me with his courtship, and offer of marriage. To a young girl, his appeal must have been irresistible.

I was also without a father. At the time, I must have felt the loss of a strong man in my life considerably. I had been brought up in a household of two women; no man had given me his presence or guidance. To myself, a young and inexperienced girl, the arrival of Ralph into my existence must have brought me both strength and courage.

No wonder I had accepted his proposal! I had had no option. Circumstances must also have prompted my decision. No doubt this was considered an ideal match. The approbation of public opinion must have been a weight too heavy to resist.

I stopped beside the river, suddenly longing to see before me the figure of Miles striding along the towpath in his crewman's gansey and breeches. But there was no one. Only myself and my own probing and relentless thoughts.

I did not love Ralph. I did not know what my emotions had been previously towards him. But now, I was sure I did not care for him with any depth or passion which would prepare me for any future life with him.

Before, I had been a girl; now, events

had formed and shaped me, and I was a woman, still young in years, however. The events of my life had been so sudden and drastic, that all periods of immaturity had been superceded, and I knew that I was now an adult, with power over my own life and my own future.

I had known that the returning of my memory would be a voyage of discovery for me, a period of self-realization and re-evaluation of myself. And I welcomed the new self-knowledge my returning health had brought.

The years ahead were mine to shape. Choices were mine, and I felt capable of making the correct decisions. I felt suddenly calmed and strengthened, and I faced the future ahead without fear.

I longed suddenly to see Miles; I knew I must meet him, and talk with him without delay.

I had much to tell him.

That I was not French in origin was a beginning! I was not even Belgian, though I had lived out my life, so far, in Bruges. But I was English by birth and family. One main obstacle which had always been in my mind, separating us had, with the arrival of Ralph, been removed.

I must tell Miles of Ralph's arrival, of course. And tell Miles also that I did not love my former fiancé. My thought and imaginings did not go beyond this point. I felt only that I must see Miles and tell him that the obstacle to our love was removed, and that I was able to love him with all my heart.

I walked back to Riverside House and entered the conservatory. Janet followed me in, and told me that Lieutenant Stanley had arrived earlier, and wished to speak to me. My heart knew no bounds in its joy at the thought of seeing Miles again.

He was still in his formal uniform as he entered the room, and I remembered he had been attending the admiralty, in London. He looked tired from his exertions, and lines of strain showed upon his face.

To my surprise, he bowed to me formally, and did not approach me to take my hand in his, and give me the kiss of salute. He stood before me very erect, withdrawn, and somehow unapproachable.

I stared at this new Miles with amazement, and felt too astonished to speak. But there was no need for me to address Miles. For he was speaking to me.

"Celeste, I have heard of the arrival from Belgium of your fiancé, Captain van de Meuve. The news has set all East Quayling agog, and naturally it reached the ears of my father's household. I must congratulate you upon being reunited with the man whom you intend to marry. I trust the ceremony is not too far off, and that all felicity will be yours."

I was still too nonplussed to speak, and indeed all power of speech seemed to have left me. Miles resumed:

"Naturally, I will stand down in my own suit regarding yourself. What a good thing it was that we had not become formally committed to one another! Our relationship was a friendship only, and had no other name or intention."

"Miles, you are totally mistaken," I said. "I pray you give me leave to speak to explain this matter, and my own implication in it."

"I feel that explanations are superfluous and might be painful to both sides," Miles said coldly. "What explanation can justify your actions in leading one man on, in a close relationship, while betrothed to another?"

"But I assure you Miles, my memory was clouded. I had no recollection of my engagement to Ralph van de Meuve."

"That is naturally your explanation," Miles said. "And one which I expected, but cannot accept. I believe your friendship with myself was an act of dalliance, to while away the time until your fiancé arrived.

"Indeed, I doubt the whole of your

loss of memory, Celeste. I think this was a ruse to give yourself a holiday in England, some new experiences and excitement, before you settled down. And you succeeded. You hoodwinked me and drew me to the edge of a proposal of marriage. If it is any matter of satisfaction to yourself to have done this, you have gained your end. But I have suffered a severe reverse, in that I have lost all faith in you as a valued friend. And my disillusion with your nature and character is deep and complete."

I had risen while Miles had been speaking, and I faced him now, and cried:

"How can you make such statements to me, after our attachment, and affection for one another? This alone, my preference for you, must have meant something, and has indicated the opposite to your accusations of deceit and ill-faith."

"I have thought deeply over my statements to you, Celeste, and I retract nothing," Miles said. "I am only glad we did not make public to others our regard for one another. To have done this, when Ralph van de Meuve arrived, would have made my humiliation complete. No doubt my disappointment and betrayal have amused you, now that the captain has returned. I ask you not to present the captain to me. Nor to be in touch with me in the future. I wish no further communication between us.

"Goodbye, Celeste. I hope never to see you again. If you honour this wish, you will best serve the interests of both you and myself. Farewell."

Miles bowed formally, and his attitude was so strict, so unyielding, so inborn I had no words to stay him. And indeed, had no wish to do so. But as I watched him go, I knew that tears stood in my eyes. I heard a voice crying with pain and regret in the conservatory. I was surprised to realize it was my own.

★ ★ ★

There is a grapevine in every family, and it was not long before everyone knew what had occurred. "I will go to see Miles," Robin said. "When he is more fully acquainted with the situation, his attitude may unbend, and he may yield from his uncompromising position."

"I beg you to do no such thing," I replied. I could not bear that anyone should approach Miles and beg for my reinstatement in his life, and his friendship. Pride would not allow such a step. The gulf between us was irrevocable, and could not be closed.

I could not help but overhear Vinnie talking to Imelda. "There is no doubt that Miles Stanley is glad to get out of his friendship with Celeste. And the return of Ralph is a good excuse! For you and I know well that Miles has been a philanderer in his time. He has led other women on before, without having any serious intention."

I thought Vinnie's tone bitter as she

193

said these words. No doubt this was how she viewed her former friendship with Miles, a friendship which I knew full well had been terminated by Miles himself.

"Also, many men seek to free themselves from an encumbrance before they are called to the colours, or are obliged to take part in warfare. I feel that Miles has rid himself of an obligation to Celeste, using the arrival of Ralph van de Meuve as justification.

"Not that Celeste is the loser!" she added. "Some women have good fortune showered upon them without stint!"

"Whatever do you mean, Vinnie?" Imelda cried. "Do you yourself admire Captain van de Meuve?"

I did not hear the answer as the two women moved away. I felt guilt in that I had heard so much, but allowed that Vinnie's reactions were not unreasonable and expectable from others as well.

After a few days, Ralph came to see me, as soon as he arrived in East Quayling from London. I saw at once that his face was pale, and his expression strained. He asked that we might be alone, and I preceded him into a small room called the morning room, which was little used at this time of day. We sat down together.

"A member of the family has told me what has occurred," Ralph began. "And believe me, I do not offer you blame, but rather sympathy and commiseration."

I looked at Ralph with surprise. I saw that his eyes were indeed earnest and sincere, and that upon his face there was an expression of understanding. "Pray clarify your statement, Ralph," I said. "I am at a loss as to the precise intent of your sympathy and concern."

"I am told that you formed an attachment with a local man, while you were residing in East Quayling," Ralph said. "And it is upon this matter that I wish to speak."

I waited, and Ralph went on. "It is no doubt due to your loss of memory that his relationship was formed. I cannot believe that you could have remembered our own engagement, and formed a liaison in addition to this."

"That is so," I admitted. "But even so . . . " I began to form the words in my mind that would tell Ralph of my deep involvement with Miles, involvement that was still intense, in spite of his rejection of me. But Ralph was speaking again.

"These small infatuations come and go often in the best regulated of lives," he said. "The mistake is to give them importance. The prudent course is to acknowledge their transience, and to admit that they have no bearing upon the ordered course of a committed and dedicated life."

I glanced at him and saw that indeed he believed my friendship with Miles to have been a flirtation only. At this moment, a storm of weeping assailed me, and in spite of all my efforts at control, I broke down and sobbed with abandon. I know that my shoulders shook with the force of my emotion, and I saw the tears run down my dress and hands.

Ralph drew me to himself. He said no words, but laid his lips upon my hair and my forehead. I felt the reassuring strength of his arm around my shoulders, and his own snowy kerchief stemmed the flood of weeping from my eyes.

"Let us put the whole of this matter behind us," Ralph said. "I know that the gentleman in question jilted you and this must have shattered your pride. But believe me, I will do all that I can to amend this situation. In my own love, care and regard for you, you will find the solace that this wound requires.

"Yet I cannot let this matter pass without a word of condemnation of the gentleman in question. I believe that to lead on an innocent girl who had lost her memory was an act of irresponsible unkindliness."

"I will not hear any ill of Miles Stanley!" I cried. "Please Ralph, do not slander him in your words or your mind!"

"You are very loyal, Celestine," Ralph replied. "Your good feelings do you credit. But I fear that ambition is the overriding emotion of the man you name. No woman can compete in his life with his ship, the *Victory*, and his dedication to the cause of Lord Nelson."

I wished to end this conversation concerning Miles and myself and said to Ralph, "Could you please give me my aunt's address, so that I myself can write to her, and tell her that I am well?"

"I will do this with pleasure, though your letter will have to travel with the Belgian diplomatic mail," Ralph said. "But this matter was early attended to. I naturally wrote to Madame la Foche as soon as I found you. She has been distraught with worry over many months, and I was anxious to let her know your whereabouts, and to put her mind at rest."

"How kind you are, Ralph!" I cried, involuntarily, and this was true. The whole of this conversation had revealed his deep sensitivity and responsible attitude. What a wonderful husband he would have made! Had not my heart been given to another who would have none of me now?

"I am anxious also on another matter, Ralph," I said. "What of Miss Preston? Where is she now?"

"Still in hospital in London, I am afraid. Her injuries were serious, and she has been immobilized."

"How has she fared? Who has visited her?"

"I myself have kept in touch with her. And a member of my staff has attended to her wants."

At this moment, before we could take the conversation further, we were joined by Imelda, who insisted that we should repair to the drawing room. Janet brought in an infusion of tea and Evan joined us, with the conversation becoming more general.

Ralph finally said: "You will know that, in January, Admiral Pierre Villeneuve escaped from Toulon, and that Lord Nelson chased him to the West Indies and back to Europe. Napoleon Bonaparte's design was simple. He planned that his fleets at Toulon and Cartagena should smash the British blockade, led by Lord Nelson, and then head for the West Indies. There, in one concentration, they would destroy both the British islands and their trade.

"Then, in one combined sweep, Napoleon's two navies would head back across the Atlantic and annihilate the British navy off Ushant. Thus, in command of the Channel, Napoleon could immediately ship well over one hundred and fifty thousand soldiers to England. The downfall and defeat of these islands would then be assured.

"But Napoleon had reckoned without

Nelson. And the spirit of resistance of the British people. Now, after several minor skirmishes, the two fleets, both French and Spanish, are at Cadiz. And so, the final reckoning approaches. Lord Nelson has been summoned by the Admiralty in London to undertake the final battle. A battle that could bring triumph for Britain, or defeat for Napoleon Bonaparte. Indeed, the alternative is slavery for the British people, or their freedom."

"And it all rests upon the shoulders of Lord Nelson," Imelda said. "And he looks so frail. He is so small, and he has only one eye and one arm! In appearance he is almost like an invalid. I am told that Lady Hamilton cossets him like a child."

"The spirit of a man transcends his infirmities," said Ralph stoutly, and it was clear that Ralph had great admiration for Lord Nelson. I remembered Miles telling me of how often Lord Nelson had been called to the Admiralty during his last days at

Merton. He had had a brief vacation in his beloved home, broken by frequent official visits to London.

I watched Ralph go with regret. Truth to tell, his generosity and his stalwart common sense had done much to ease the inevitable pain of my mind. I realized that I had not told him of my changed personal feelings towards him. Yet he had been so kind to me, I shrank from causing him further pain.

I would tell him on a suitable occasion in the future, I promised myself. But as for now . . . I rested in his strength and reassurance; I drew solace from his comfort. He had aided me at a difficult time in my life, and I was grateful to him, and thankful for his friendship and support.

* * *

During the time of these personal events, matters had progressed, or altered, at Riverside House.

Imelda was forging ahead with

preparations for her marriage, and seemed happy with her private preoccupations. She still felt regret about her inability to bear a child, but the sharing of the situation had drawn Robin and herself closer together. She now accepted her lot without outward grieving or fuss.

But Evan had withdrawn into himself, and seemed to have no spirit for life, or energy or enjoyment in the pursuits which had beguiled him previously.

Vinnie remained true to her own nature, her personality fluctuating like the wind. Kindly at one moment, acid the next. I was certain it had been she who had informed Ralph of the events with Miles.

Vinnie was still officially in a state of courtship with Evan, yet the state seemed to bring neither of them satisfaction or joy. I sometimes wondered if Vinnie had begun to hanker after Miles again. A fruitless longing! For Miles had now quit East Quayling and had gone to join his ship, the *Victory*, at Portsmouth. I thought that Ralph's words might be true, that with the approaching battle, Miles would have dismissed all women from his mind. The one guiding star of his existence now would be his chief, Admiral Nelson.

It was inevitable that soon Ralph would press me to return to Bruges. "Truth to tell, Celestine, I should be glad to know that you were out of the danger zone. For believe me, with this naval battle to come, every person in England will be in jeopardy, and no one will know from one day to the next, if and when disaster will befall."

"But I understood that the sea crossing is difficult now, Ralph, in view of Lord Nelson's instruction to clear the Channel approaches."

"The Belgian Government has a fast steamer for use of diplomatic personnel, and I am certain you could cross the Channel in the safety of this vessel. Please do give the matter thought, Celestine. I am anxious for you, and anxious also about our future."

"But before I go to Bruges, there is someone in England I must see," I answered.

"And who is that?" Ralph questioned kindly.

"Miss Preston. I feel that I must travel to London to see Miss Preston in hospital, without delay. After all, she was with me when we were first attacked. She has clearly suffered more serious harm than myself, since she is still in nursing care. Can you arrange this, Ralph? I feel strongly that I must see Miss Preston before I do anything more."

This desire was expressed to the rest of the family. To my surprise Robin Marchmant said thoughtfully:

"I have a house in London. My father loved the social life of the city, and often lived for quite long spells at this house in Cavendish Square. As for myself — I prefer the country. But the house is still furnished, and has a housekeeper. She and her husband reside on the premises, attend to its upkeep, and keep the dwelling ready for occupation. "So I propose that we all adjourn to London for a holiday.

"Ralph, this will be more convenient for you to see Celeste. It is clearly a strain for you to keep journeying into the country, when your embassy is situated in London. Imelda, you can choose some furnishings for Claremont Hall, and your own wedding dress, my dear. Evan, you adore London and have many friends there. And Vinnie . . . "

"Yes, I would like to come too," Vinnie said. "A change of scene can often mean a change of fortune," she added, rather sagely, I thought.

"And Celeste . . . you can see Miss Preston, and can await that fast packet to Bruges."

And so it was arranged. So easily and competently as Robin always arranged things. But one thought came unbidden into my mind, and remained there, and would not go away.

In London, in that city of several thousand souls were two people I desperately wanted to encounter.

In London lived Mrs. Magwich and Robert Lessing. And I knew that I was dedicated to discovering their whereabouts, and that I was determined to do all that I could to bring them to justice at last.

# 9

LONDON astounded me. The height of the buildings was amazing. Some were three or four stories high! The speed of the horses drawing the carriages, the rattle of wheels on stones, the variety of the shops, the throng of the pedestrians ... The whole panorama took my breath away. It was several days before I could assimilate the change, and become accustomed to the dizzy rate and stress of city life.

"Yes indeed, the pace of life is very rapid in the capital, Celeste," Robin told me. "You can see from the expressions on the faces of passersby that the pressure of life takes its toll. I am told that clergymen regularly preach from their pulpits the dangers of this tension-filled life. East Quayling, and no doubt Bruges, were havens of peace compared to this."

Yet I loved to go out into the city, and accompany Imelda on her excursions, as she bought her trousseau and additional furnishings for Claremont Hall. However, some of the sights and sounds of London oppressed and saddened me.

Poverty was rife and beggars abounded. Little children roamed free without supervision, nor, apparently did they have homes. Many people tried to drown their difficulties in drink and besotted tramps lurched from side to side, while the police tried to clear a path. Ladies of the night accosted customers quite brazenly, and many piteous women begged openly for their children and themselves.

"There is much to be done," Evan said. He seemed touched by these evidences of poverty and distress. "No wonder my uncle is so moved to give his aid to these necessitous cases."

This was the first time that Evan had spoken of his uncle for a long time.

"Please invite Uncle Edmund round to dinner, Evan," Imelda said. "We must entertain him now that we are in the city."

I looked forward to seeing Lord Stanhope again. But as I trod the city streets with Imelda, or other members of the family, my thoughts were elsewhere. For somewhere, within this city, hidden among these thousands of anonymous people, were those I sought. Somewhere in London were Mrs. Magwich and Robert Lessing.

In vain I scanned the crowds, the passersby, the shoppers, the habitués of coffee houses and those issuing from inns. But I did not see them. They are here in London I told myself — my assailants, and also, unfortunately, custodians of other innocent young victims of their trade.

I examined the terraces of houses, the squares, the streets, the roads, seeking some slight sign which I might have noticed during the night when I had fled from their premises. Yet I saw nothing that awoke memories; all was unfamiliar. But I did not give up hope, or cease my observations. I was certain that, with Evan in London, they would reveal themselves to me.

Yes, Evan was the bait. He was the one who would lure them from their hiding place. I did not doubt but that they would contact him, in time. Thus, in addition to my scrutiny of London Streets, I also placed Evan under my observation. Somewhere, sometime they would contact him, and I would do my best to pick up some hint, some clue as to their whereabouts. I had every intention of tracking them to their lair.

There was a little delay in gaining permission for me to visit the hospital in which Miss Preston was lodged. In spite of Ralph's depositions to the authorities, permission was not at first granted. Later, I learned that a case of cholera had alerted the nursing staff, so that visiting was halted.

Meanwhile, the whole family had

settled into the house in Cavendish Square. To my surprise, this was a narrow terrace house with a black front door, and railings fencing off a basement.

Yet in spite of its deceptive size, the dwelling had many rooms, all furnished and ready for occupation. We all had a single room, and Mr. and Mrs. Bennett, the staff, were delighted to be of service, and happy to find the town house occupied again.

Lord Stanhope came to dinner, and charmed us all with his stories of Venice. He paid particular attention to Evan, whose diffident attitude towards his uncle relaxed a little as they conversed together.

How I longed that Evan would confide in his uncle, so that the police might be informed of the whereabouts of Mrs. Magwich and Robert! How much simpler it would have made my present and future course! But Evan kept his silence. He cherished his future inheritance above all else. I noticed that

Evan went out little, now that we were in London, and his gambling haunts and former companions knew him no more.

Ralph came to see us frequently. "Naturally, I am delighted to have your company in London," he told me. "I am obliged to visit Portsmouth frequently, where the British fleet is assembling, and where Lord Nelson's flagship, the *Victory*, is being provisioned for the coming battle."

He paused. We were in the small front sitting room. Outside, the cries of London echoed, lavender sellers, muffin men, the shouts of itinerant hawkers. He took my hand in his.

"You are looking better in health, Celestine, since you arrived in London," he said. "I regret the delay in visiting Miss Preston, yet the respite seems to have done you good." He paused, yet I scarcely heard him. For at the mention of the ship *Victory*, the memory of Miles filled my mind.

He was never far from my thoughts,

and indeed my recollections of him filled my waking hours. I doubted that I would ever see him again, yet this did not lessen my caring for him; absence and separation had not altered my love for him. That was affixed in my mind as a star — the guiding light of my life — and yet I knew that it would lead me nowhere.

As if he knew my thoughts, Ralph said, "As soon as the blockade is lifted, and we can return to Bruges, I am sure your unhappy memories will be put behind you.

"Unhappy memories for myself also," he added after a pause. "For I cannot bear to see you distressed. I have loved you for so long, that I cannot believe my devotion will go unrewarded, I yearn for the fulfillment of our love in marriage and the bonding of our two lives together."

I should have told him then, I realized that now, that my heart was still given to Miles. Yet I hoped, in a despairing kind of way, that Ralph's devotion might stimulate a return of my former affection.

And his devotion was a comfort. I felt often grieved by Miles' dismissal of me. To have Ralph's approval and attention healed some of the wounds in my heart. He had become a vital and honoured part of my life.

It was clearly also expected by all my friends that now, with Miles gone, I should resume my engagement to Ralph. He was gladly received by the household. All of the old hostility to him had vanished; he was almost as one of the family now, welcomed and approved. And he, in his turn, gave to us a thoughtful attention that added to all our lives.

I was glad when Ralph called one day at the house in Cavendish Square, to inform me that visiting was now in order at the hospital, and that I could see Miss Preston that very day.

Imelda accompanied me as far as the vestibule of St. Jude's Hospice. From there I was directed to the ward in which my former governess lay.

I was later to learn that this was a model hospital, yet to me it appeared a hotbed of chaos and neglect.

Huge, burly nurses attended to the patients; beds were few, and many patients lay upon palliasses on the floor.

Bed coverings were scanty. Dressings were unchanged. Many of the visitors were plying the patients with gin and other spirits. I wondered how many of these unfortunates ever left this hospice alive. Reforms were so obviously needed.

But my guide directed me to a more salubrious part of the hospital, where patients whose relatives could afford to pay the somewhat more exorbitant fees, were lodged. I walked down the long corridor, towards a room at the end of the passage. Here the air was fresh and clean, and in the room at the end of the walk I could see . . .

And then I was running down the corridor, my skirts flying, my bonnet blown to the winds, the combs spilling out of my hair. My arms were stretched out before me, I heard my voice echoing in the bare and empty passage.

For I could see Miss Preston in the narrow bed in the room ahead. But in addition to Miss Preston, sitting beside the bed of my governess was the figure of a lady, instantly recognizable, perfectly recollected, and loved. For sitting beside Miss Preston was my aunt, Madame la Foche, from Bruges.

* * *

"Aunt Adelaide!" I was crying. "Aunt Adelaide . . ." And then I had reached the small ward, and had clasped my relation in my arms.

I felt the warmth of her frame, the rounded plumpness of her figure and the softness of her cheek as I saluted her. I smelled her perfume, a distillation of floral odours from Paris. I saw her gray hair, curling in the nape of her neck beneath her brocaded hat with plumes. And then we were both crying, both standing beside Miss Preston's bed with the tears coursing down our cheeks. It seemed that we could never end our embrace.

"Celestine! How I have craved to see you! All these months and days. I have prayed. I have longed for your safety! And now you are here, clearly none the worse for your experience. Let me look at you again, for I never thought to see you more. Dear Celestine. Welcome home." And again my aunt clasped me in her loving arms.

My aunt, Madame la Foche, was a lady of style and spirit, without being too addicted to the passing mode. She had a manner all her own, and seemed to add luster to whatever she wore, and to the occasion.

"But here is Miss Preston," my aunt was saying. "She also has worried about you, although grievously troubled by afflictions of her own." And I turned from the sight of my beloved aunt's face, and regarded Miss Preston.

218

Louise Preston was small and neat, with a face and features like an inquisitive bird. She had dark hair, now braided about her head. She was sitting up in bed. Her back and shoulders were still strapped with bandages, yet she seemed in good spirits, and able to bear her misfortune.

"Dearest Celestine." Tears did not stand in her indomitable eyes, but her voice broke as she held my hand in her free hand. "That you are safe after all this time! And you escaped from the dreadful place to where you were abducted. I blame myself," the governess went on, "that I was not more aware of the dangers of this cruel city. I am sure nothing of the kind would have befallen you in Brussels. Belgium is safer than England, at any time. I blame this permissive age," Miss Preston continued. "The crown prince sets a bad example, with his women. And the poor king is forgetful, and does not concern himself with morals." She sighed. "Be that as it may, we are reunited at last. And all that remains to do, is for me to recover my health, so that we can return to Bruges, and take up our lives again in the Harbour House."

I thought that Aunt Adelaide eyed me shrewdly as Miss Preston made her last remark. It was as if she guessed that other plans might have entered my mind, during my stay in England. But nothing was said, and the moment passed. In any case, I thought, my plans to stay in England had all gone awry. I had been given my congé, and there was no mistake about that.

I gave Miss Preston the gifts I had brought her, some powder of orrisroot, a book of romance, and a phial of eau-de-cologne. "How did you manage to enter England?" I asked my aunt. "And when did you arrive?"

"I came into Tilbury on the last boat from Bruges to London. As you will know, all sea passages are now closed.

"And Ralph arranged it for me.

He has been a tower of strength, Celestine. He had paid for Miss Preston's treatment in this private part of the hospital, and he visited her when he could. I cannot speak too highly of him, Celestine.

"Naturally, he informed us when he had traced you to East Quayling, but he advised against my visiting you there.

"He said there was some kind of trouble, and he feared that any further shocks might have a deleterious result.

"Of course, I abided by his advice, and have awaited you in London. I have taken lodgings, nearby, and have visited Miss Preston daily. I knew it was only a matter of time before we were united again."

"Please tell us, now that we are reunited, what happened to you, and the events of the past few months," Miss Preston said.

I began to tell my aunt and Miss Preston of the occurrences in my recent life. I did not mention Miles, naturally, but I told the two ladies of the wonderful kindness I had received at Riverside House in East Quayling.

I recounted the incident in the street market, when I had heard the young couple mention East Quayling. "Some memory stirred," I said. "Something prompted me to seek safety in this village.

"I heard this name mentioned in the bordello, and unconsciously I desired to make my way there."

Miss Preston looked at me quizzically and smiled. "But the words East Quayling were already imprinted upon your mind," she said. "I myself was born in East Quayling, and brought up there. I often mentioned this village to you, Celestine, and told you anecdotes of the life there. So you see . . . In spite of the blow upon your head, you recognized the name. East Quayling offered a refuge to you. It was no accident that you made your way there."

At this moment the head of the

hospital entered and informed all visitors that they must leave. I said goodbye to Miss Preston with reluctance, for I knew I had had great affection for her, that she had given me my education as a child before becoming companion and aide to Madame la Foche.

Indeed, she clung to me a little, and tears stood in her eyes. I held her in my arms, and then left the pathetic figure with regret.

★ ★ ★

Imelda was still in the foyer. I introduced the two ladies, and we all repaired to Aunt Adelaide's lodgings, where cakes and an infusion of tea were served.

I returned back to Cavendish Square with Imelda, for this arrangement had been agreed upon, and I felt happier than I had for some time. I had found my aunt; I had discovered my roots and my family. And what is more, with the coming of my aunt, a further section of my memory had returned.

I am quite unable to explain this, and indeed, doubt that this phenomenon has any rational or medical explanation. But with the sight of Miss Preston and Aunt Adelaide, not only buildings, not only sights and sounds returned, but the memory of people flooded back to my mind.

And I knew the joy of remembering the face and form of my beloved father again. I recalled my childhood playmates, the neighbours at the Harbour House, my friends, the shopkeepers, the launderer, even the mendicants who had haunted the quay, and the seamen who had walked its stones.

I felt a sudden surge of satisfaction and a deep sense of gratitude filled my being. Small wonder I could not face the opera that night.

Ralph had asked me to accompany him to a rendition of a French musical play which he particularly wished to see. But now . . . "I beg you to excuse me, please, Ralph." I said. I told him what had occurred, and he was overjoyed for me. "But do not waste the box which you have taken," I added. "Why not take Vinnie in my place? She has not been out very much lately, and I am sure she would welcome a visit to Covent Garden."

Ralph agreed rather reluctantly, I thought, although Vinnie hastened off to make her toilet. It was true, she had not been out a great deal since our arrival in London. Evan, her beau, had not wished to enter social life, and Vinnie's pleasure had been somewhat restricted.

I watched them go; they made a charming couple, I thought. Ralph so tall and handsome, and Vinnie, petite and elegant. He handed her into the carriage with his usual polish and charm. They bowed and I waved. Then I returned to my own thoughts.

If only Miles were here, so that I could tell him what had occurred! Only he was missing from my life.

The remembrances of our brief hours together returned to me with shattering force. It seemed that the recovery of memory brought as much pain as forgetfulness.

My memory had returned, certainly, there was no doubt about that. Yet not entirely. There was still an area of doubt and hesitation in my mind.

One piece of my memory was missing still. But what this fragment of recollection was, I did not know. And how it would reveal itself, and the results of this revelation, were hidden from me too. Only time would tell, and I must await the future and events with all the calmness and optimism of which I was capable.

# 10

THE next day, the house in Cavendish Square was in ferment, for Ralph proposed that on the morrow we should all accompany him to Portmouth to see Lord Nelson's flagship the *Victory*.

"Crowds of people from all over England will be flocking to see this vessel, before it leaves the harbour. It is dressed overall, and without doubt it is a spectacle not to be missed. I can provide the conveyance, for I have some official business to transact and have an official vehicle at my disposal. There is room for everyone, and I will also provide the picnic luncheon. An early start will be essential, so may I beg of you to be prepared by eight o'clock."

Later this same day, I went to see my aunt at the lodgings in Eaton Place.

She had a very pleasant suite of rooms, and she was sufficiently settled. Miss Preston had been released from the hospital, and was resting in the sitting room upon a chaise longue.

At the moment, she was being visited by a young medical man called Doctor Meredith, and his wife, who was a trained nurse. They attended to Miss Preston in my presence, and I was greatly impressed by their expertise and their kindly approach.

My aunt took me aside, as Miss Preston dozed, and began to speak to me seriously. "I beg you to tell me, Celestine, what has happened concerning your engagement to Ralph? I gather that all is not well, and it is expedient that I should know the truth."

I told my aunt gladly that during my loss of memory I had met, and had come to care deeply for Miles Stanley.

I told her also of Miles' dismissal of me, and the intense hurt this had caused my feelings. I stated that my relationship now with Ralph was that of a stalemate. I did not love him as before, yet I hoped my love for him would return, since I respected and honoured him deeply as a person. I had no wish to cause needless hurt by a dismissal of Ralph before I was entirely sure of my feelings.

I mentioned the sense of opposition I had felt concerning my engagement to Ralph, and my aunt smiled.

"There was opposition indeed, all the time, and from the start."

She explained, "Madame van de Meuve, Ralph's mother, opposed the match strenously, and did all she could to end the engagement. You see, we are not wealthy, Celestine. Your father left you a sufficiency for a moderate style of life in his will. This, allied to my own income, has been enough for our household in Bruges.

"Yet Madame van de Meuve wished for a large dowry with Ralph's wife. She was hoping that he would marry a wealthy woman, and a Belgian also. Your British nationality did not please her, and was regarded as an impediment in her sight.

"I do not go so far as to say that she was pleased by your disappearance," my aunt said cautiously. "But I was told she is not overjoyed by your return. Therefore, Ralph has had to undergo opposition from his mother for his steadfast attachment to you and his wish to marry you.

"I personally believe that Ralph has shown great courage in his continued defense of you, Celestine. He naturally honours his mother, as any man would, but seeks to reserve the right to choose his future wife for himself.

"I urge you, therefore, to think twice before you end your engagement to Ralph. He has proved himself to you, doubly, by his search for you and by his concern for you now. And by his persistence in his championing of you in spite of his mother's opposition. It may be that your falling in love with

Miles Stanley was a figment of your imagination only, Celestine, brought on by your disturbed state of mind, and your lack of stability and feeling of disorientation."

My aunt paused, then added, "Give yourself time, as you are doing, before you reach any decision. To accept a man's love is often the first step towards loving him in return. Enjoy the picnic tomorrow. I am certain that you have taken the correct course so far, and that the future will prove both of us to be right."

I returned to Cavendish Square in a thoughtful mood. But my considerations were not entirely of myself and my own situation.

"Imelda," I said. "I have met a clever young man, Doctor Meredith, who, my aunt informs me, specializes in matters concerning the female form.

"He is aided by his wife, who is a midwife and skilled in disorders of the female constitution. May I ask, indeed beg of you, to seek an interview with this young medical couple, and ask for an examination of the trouble which has so blighted your life? It is a long time ago since you had your first examination. I am told that medical science is progressing, and that these two young people are in the forefront of this new knowledge. Please Imelda, think this over. I will, of course, accompany you on the first consultation, if you wish."

Imelda was at first taken aback by my suggestion. Then she said, "I will consider this matter, and give you my reply when we return from Portsmouth. I can hardly dare to hope, yet you have given me fresh courage, Celeste."

It was a beautiful day in early September when Ralph's carriage drew up at the house in Cavendish Square, and we all set off for our visit to Portsmouth.

It was naturally the expected thing that Ralph and I should sit together. Imelda and Robin were close together, and Vinnie and Evan also were paired off in an acceptable way. We appeared to be a party of affianced couples journeying on a day's excursion. I think we gave no sign of the tensions which were occupying us all.

As it so often happens in September, it seemed that the quintessence of summer enwrapped us. The trees moved gently as the carriage with its powerful team of horses took us swiftly through the countryside. The fields sped by; the houses and cottages were glimpsed, and then passed. The sun gave a brilliance to the scene and the scent of cottage flowers flew into our carriage, as we left the capital far behind and headed for the coast.

And now, a more salty air assailed us. We were approaching the sea. Ralph had made this journey in his official conveyance many times, and he pointed out different objects of interest to us as we approached Portsmouth.

I was a little silent during this journey, for my aunt's information and opinions had affected me deeply. Also

Evan's own silence and preoccupation caused me concern.

It was as if, because their own partners were strangely silent, that Vinnie and Ralph began to talk together. Vinnie asked Ralph many eager questions, and he replied in his open and forthright way. I had not seen Vinnie sparkle so much for a long time, and I guessed that her conversation eased private matters in Ralph's mind.

I was unprepared for the size of Portsmouth; its dimensions astonished me, and it was thronged with people, and not only seafarers and sailors. It seemed that all the populace from nearby had congregated at the port where Lord Nelson's ship lay, and from which he was soon to make his departure to join the fleet.

On the approaches to the docks, it was like a fair. A carnival atmosphere hung over everything. There were sellers of various wares, eatables, sweetmeats, and the like.

A brisk trade was being done in emblems, which sailors could present to the girls of their choice before their departures overseas. And in return, there were tokens of affection and remembrance from the girls to their sailor friends.

This brisk trade and the sellers pushing around the crowd gave a ferment to the throng of bystanders, who were pressing up to the railings around the docks. The noise was terrific — the cries, the badinage, the teasing, the reckless promises, the sad moans of farewell! One could have been lost and trampled underfoot, had not a steady head been kept. And a tight hand upon one's purse, for there were many thieves in this crowd, plying their trade of plunder and fraud.

At last, Ralph somehow made a way through this throng — perhaps aided by his very official naval uniform — and we all assembled at the railings of the docks. Before us lay the harbour of Portsmouth and further away, the flagship of the British navy, the *Victory*.

She was certainly dressed overall, and her paintwork and decorations were immaculate. We could see the crewmen busy about their tasks upon the decks. Yet there was an air of readiness about this huge vessel. It was as if all the preliminary labours had been done, and the crew awaited only the arrival of their commander in chief, and his word to set loose their sails upon their course.

A wave of patriotism swept through me. How glad I was to be of English nationality, and by right, a part of this stirring scene! This was my country, which Lord Nelson and his fleet were sailing to protect. My heart filled with pride. I regretted only that my own father was absent, for he too would have rejoiced to see this naval vessel prepared for sea.

"It is now September the tenth," Ralph told me. "On Sunday September the 15th, Lord Nelson will set sail.

"He will take command of the fleet

off Cadiz shortly after this. I trust all will go well with him," Ralph continued thoughtfully. "Lord Nelson is, after all, approaching forty-seven years of age, and has serious disabilities in his physical health. But he has a stout servant aboard the *Victory*, one Tom Allen, who organizes his life at sea. And Doctor Beatty is a friend as well as a colleague, who cares for his health. Also, his old shipmate, Admiral Hardy, will be at his side."

"But these factors of his disabilities have not weighed with Lord Nelson for a considerable time," Robin Marchment interposed.

"It is with his spirit that he will fight this war. He is out to defeat his old enemy, Villeneuve. He will not rest until he has sunk the French fleet, or brought their ships to surrender. Lord Nelson will fight to the end, and to him there is only one end, and that is a British victory."

I saw now that the *Victory* was low in the water, stocked with supplies, and I could see her guns polished and uncovered. I saw also, that at the foot of the steps of this pier, was a barge. And within this barge were naval personnel, with their oars upright, stiff in the air, as was the custom when the vessel awaited its passenger.

Then suddenly, burly sailors were clearing a way through the crowds, and we saw a group of men approach the steps. There were six naval officers and in the front walked their commander in chief, Lord Nelson.

He walked easily through the crowd, appearing not to observe their scufflings, with his uncovered eye. The sleeve of his amputated arm was pinned across his jacket. I saw the gold braid of his uniform and that his officer's hat was worn at rather an unofficial angle.

He did not smile or acknowledge anyone, yet his progress was without ostentation of display. He might have been walking across the imaginary poop in the gardens at Merton, where I had last observed him. One almost thought to see Lady Hamilton and little Horatia, nearby. He walked calmly down the steps towards the barge, his actions cool, without excitement, and most serene.

There was an air of inevitability about him that affected all who observed this scene. Many eyes were moist, some ladies wrung their hands. Even the men fell silent. And then gradually, suddenly, the crowd began to murmur; applause rose in the air. A thunderous cheer rang out over the harbour; the people in the crowd were in a fever of agitation. Their voices semed to shake the very heavens as they honoured their hero, the man who personified their country, and who would defend their own honour to the end.

"He is with his weaponry officers," Ralph whispered to me, as the six officers followed their commander down the steps. And sure enough, a short way behind Lord Nelson, I saw the figure of Miles Stanley. They had reached the landing stage and approached the barge; in a few moments they would be gone from me forever.

I looked at Miles as if to implant the memory of his face and form upon my mind. I saw his tall figure, his lean yet sinewy build. I thought his face was paler than usual. He appeared strained, in concentration, dedicated. And then suddenly, he raised his eyes to the crowd on the pier above him, and for one moment his eyes met mine.

We looked at one another. There was the flash of recognition; yet neither made a move. Miles could not acknowledge me, nor could I bring myself to raise my hand towards him. Our eyes were locked together for a brief fraction of time, and then he looked away. He had stepped into the barge with the other officers, who had taken their positions around the area reserved for Lord Nelson.

Amidst tumultuous applause, the barge began to pull away from the pier. I saw the waters move, the action of the oars, the motions of the vessel.

The barge headed toward the *Victory*, which awaited their coming. The crowd had fallen silent now, as if they knew the occasion was too momentous for noise. Some turned from the scene, as if the moment was almost too much for them to bear.

Ralph began to lead us away towards his carriage, which had been left in an area reserved for other diplomats and high officials. The coachman began to unpack the picnic meal, but I felt I could neither eat nor drink.

For in that one moment of time, when my eyes had met Miles Stanley's, and we had gazed fully into each other's inner consciousness, my fate had been sealed, my mind made up, and my life, forever, irrevocably changed.

# 11

AT the end of our excursion to Portsmouth, I asked Ralph if I might see him privately the next day, and of course he agreed to this. We arranged that he should call at the house in Cavendish Square in the late afternoon, when his duties at the embassy were finished.

There were a few trees in the centre of Cavendish Square, and one or two stout benches, much used by wayfarers. We strolled in the square, and then, since the place was not greatly frequented, took our places upon a bench beneath an overhanging tree.

The late September air was pleasant, as it had been yesterday, and for a few moments this teeming metropolis of London had the comparative quietude of Bruges or East Quayling, a village which I knew would for ever stay in the forefront of my mind.

Ralph knew that the matter upon which I wished to speak was important. He held his peace and waited for me to speak.

I told him quite frankly, but with kindliness and consideration, that I knew that I did not love him, and that there was no possibility of our lives being united or of our future being spent together.

I thought he paled a little as I spoke, and yet he appeared not too surprised. "Is this your final decision, Celestine?" he asked me. "You know my own beliefs, expressed to you in East Quayling. That the infatuation which seized you when your memory was unhinged will disappear once we have returned to Bruges, and begin our usual life there, again."

"I shall not change," I said. "Please do not press me, Ralph. My mind is quite made up. I could not bear to see you refute my decision, and continue, as we have been, in a state of uncertainty and futile hope."

"I appreciate your thought, Celestine," he said. "But my concern in wishing to finalize our engagement has been not entirely for myself, but for your benefit also.

"What is your future to be? I know now you care for another. But does he care for you?"

"That is the crux of the whole matter," I told Ralph sadly. "He is gone from me, never to return."

"It is clearly Miles Stanley, is it not, who still claims your affection, my dear?"

"It is Miles. What you termed infatuation has become a deep and steadfast love. For myself, there is no turning back in the placing of my affections."

"But if he does not return your preference, Celestine, what is your future course? I receive the impression that he jilted you without ceremony. And I am told that this is not the first time this has occurred."

"Be that as it may," I said. "Miles' previous reputation does not affect my present resolution. It is certain that I shall not marry Miles, for he has given me my dismissal, and is ready to sail with Lord Nelson. I shall marry no one else, Ralph. Since I cannot marry Miles, I shall marry no one."

"But how can you make so fateful a decision, on such slender evidence!" cried Ralph. "You have had no communication with Miles Stanley since he left East Quayling, I know that. You saw him yesterday, but no words passed, you did not meet."

When I did not respond, he continued: "How can you, a mere slip of a girl, condemn yourself to celibacy on such slim circumstances, on so slight an attachment! This shows your innocence and lack of experience, my dear. I assure you that in time your wounds will heal, and you will love again, and this time with purpose and intent. Can you not believe me? Will you not allow me to wait for this strange passion to pass, and for you to emerge into a more mature and worldly-wise frame of mind?"

"You have waited long enough, Ralph," I told my former suitor. "And I have waited too. Waited for love to be born again. But this has not happened. And I know it will never happen now."

"So this is your final word," Ralph said sadly.

I nodded. I remembered my aunt's words. For if a man may choose his own life partner without pressure from another, so also, I told myself, should a woman. As I stood up to go, I felt free of an immense burden.

"I must ask you to excuse me from attendance at Robin's house," Ralph said. "I have an urgent business matter to attend to during the next few days."

This upset me, and he saw.

"This is not pique, Celestine. This is not sourness at my removal from your life. You have spoken to me frankly, and I accept your words and decision, but when a fleet sails for a battle, there is much to do in diplomatic circles. I know that several appointments have been written in for me."

I watched him go; the tall figure in the Belgian naval uniform crossed the square, and passed Robin's house. I saw the tight curls of his fair hair beneath his naval hat; his stride was long and bold, and he moved with decision. He was a man of sensibility and honour, and I had rejected him forever.

★ ★ ★

And now, this was clearly the point when I should have returned to Bruges with my Aunt Adelaide and Miss Preston. But since the authorities had frozen all movements of passenger ships and there was no way that we could quit England's shores, we were unwilling captives in our native land.

Miss Preston was making rapid progress in the care of Doctor Meredith and his wife and I spent much time with her. She was an interesting person in her own right. Her observations on life were forthright, and often deeply perceptive and amusing.

Aunt Adelaide and Imelda had struck up a firm friendship. Aunt Adelaide had, of course, proffered to pay Imelda a lump sum for my long stay at Riverside House, but this had been rejected, as before.

"She has become a member of the family," Imelda said. "One does not seek payment for those one cares for. Do you know that she aided me in a delicate matter concerning my engagement to Robin? And she has offered to help me again, and I have decided to accept her suggestion."

And so it was that Imelda attended the small but spotlessly clean clinic which the two young medical people had set up near to Cavendish Square. I accompanied Imelda, as I had promised to do, and waited for her in the anteroom, when she entered for her examination. This took longer than I expected.

That the treatment had been painful was clear, when Imelda joined me. Doctor Meredith accompanied her into the anteroom.

"I have attempted to manipulate the organs maladjusted by Miss Terry's fall of years ago," he said. "I do not know yet whether this procedure has been successful, but it should help her to conceive a child."

Robin's carriage took us both home, where Imelda rested in bed. We both felt encouraged by the doctor's words, but no one knew how things would turn out.

★ ★ ★

And now, in the broader sphere, Lord Nelson took over the command of the British fleet off Cadiz on the 28th day of September, 1805. It was the day before his forty-seventh birthday.

On his birthday, fifteen captains of

the fleet dined with him on the *Victory*, and he explained his tactics, how he planned to advance in two divisions, and to force Villeneuve to accept a pitched battle.

This new maneuver, this display of confidence and strength, was to be called, in future, 'the Nelson touch'. It invigorated all who heard him expound his aims, and gave new direction and vigour to his fleet.

I could not help but feel intense interest in the coming naval battle, since the man I loved was aboard the flagship, and vitally concerned. But news was hard to come by, and rumour was rife.

I was, therefore, very pleased when one day Robin brought Judge Stanley to the house in Cavendish Square. They had met in a coffeehouse, and Robin had insisted that the Judge should accompany him home to supper.

The Judge greeted me cordially, and gave no sign that he knew of the rift between Miles and myself. He listened with great attention as I told him of my seeing my aunt and Miss Preston again. His attitude was one of friendship towards the whole family, and I felt warmed that I was included in his favour and regard.

After the meal, he gave us news of the battle. "I am told that Villeneuve has already left Cadiz with eighteen French ships, and fifteen from Spain. Lord Nelson has twenty-seven ships of the line. He is outnumbered certainly; but not outclassed in spirit, experience and strategy. We can only await the outcome of the battle, when the ships confront each other. That will be the testing time for Lord Nelson, his navy and his men, and, indeed, for this country. For us all."

I longed to ask the Judge if he had had news of Miles, but dared not utter the name of the man I so dearly loved. "Have you news of Miles, sir?" asked Evan. And I awaited the Judge's reply.

"A letter came ashore before the fleet

left for Cadiz. He was well, then, and in good spirits. Working hard, which was expected of him, and for which he was ready. As soon as Admiral Nelson requires guns, Miles and his brother officers will respond with energy and efficiency.

"He mentioned Lord Nelson's dinner party, at which the admiral had enquired after the wives and families of each man. He had obtained news of loved ones, and astonished his men by revealing to them information about their homes. Miles said the occasion was deeply affecting to all present.

"Never before has a naval commander in Chief been concerned for the welfare and well-being of his men. He is the same towards the enlisted sailors, and will chat with the humblest midshipman. He is revered, even adored by the crews of his ships. They await his signals, and will honour his instructions with their very lives."

I too felt deeply affected by these words. Soon after this, Judge Stanley left. I knew that he loved Miles dearly — his only son, and indeed his only relative. I longed to offer him comfort, and had to restrain myself to hide my feelings. Perhaps the Judge knew of my emotions, for I thought he was particularly kind, and he pressed my hand as he said farewell.

And now, the preparations for the wedding of Robin and Imelda were progressing apace. "It is almost time we returned to East Quayling," Imelda told me. "Will you accompany us, or will you stay in London, Celeste? The choice is yours, my dear. I hope only that you will attend my wedding for I could not think of marrying Robin without you by my side."

"I think I must remain in London," I answered thoughtfully. But I did not tell Imelda the reason why I must remain in the capital, at least until it was time for me to return to Bruges.

For never far from my thoughts had been the matter concerning Mrs. Magwich and Robert Lessing. Although other events had occupied my life, my wish and desire to apprehend them had not lost its importance or urgency. But so far they had not revealed themselves to me.

In a circumspect way I observed Evan. We had become firm friends, almost like an affectionate brother and his sister. I felt concern for him, for he seemed almost in a state of decline.

It was clear that his romance with Vinnie was almost over; Vinnie seemed to have lost interest in him, and she had thrown herself into the pleasure of London life.

Yet there were few places where she could go unaccompanied. I was therefore surprised to see her, one evening, preparing herself to go out. Her costume was elaborate in the extreme, and her hair had been dressed professionally, and ornamented with silver-studded combs, and wings of osprey.

Her expression was a little shamefaced when she met me on the stairs. "I am going to a reception at the Belgian Embassy with Ralph," she told me. "He has invited me to be his guest."

"I trust you will not think I am trespassing on your friendship, Celeste," she told me, with unexpected humility. "But I understand . . . That Ralph is free now. And you yourself . . . "

"Please do not be embarrassed, Vinnie," I replied. "I am happy that you have been asked out to the reception. And Ralph is a charming companion." I helped her to adjust her wrap, and she awaited Ralph's arrival in the hall.

Evan had struck up a friendship with a young lady who lived near Cavendish Square. I believe that she was a milliner, or apprenticed to a modiste. I had seen them chatting together in the Square, and I felt glad that her vivacious conversation was pleasing and helpful to Evan. Her name was Candide; she often strolled purposefully through the Square, in the hope of seeing Evan. He had not introduced her into the house, but I had the feeling that they were meeting elsewhere.

Mrs. Magwich and Robert had not been in touch with Evan lately, of that I was sure. Evan was short of money; his allowance was long since spent. But his uncle, Lord Stanhope, called at the house in Cavendish Square one day, and asked that Evan should accompany him to a museum which he wished to survey. Lord Stanhope was considering financial aid for this institution, and he thought that Evan could help him make up his mind.

I do not know the outcome of this excursion, whether the museum was helped or not, but Lord Stanhope certainly reimbursed Evan for his time and trouble. So that, at this particular time, Evan had money in his pocket, and was certainly in a better frame of mind.

I was alone a great deal during these days, and I felt my solitude keenly.

Everyone in my immediate circle

seemed to have a friend or loved one. Only I was the odd one out, with no one to turn to, or upon whom to focus my time and attention.

I spent a great deal of time at the house in Eaton Place, where my aunt and Miss Preston were lodged. Miss Preston was greatly improved in health, and they made several excursions to places of interest in the capital.

Louise Preston had also become very attached to Vinnie and saw in her tart tongue, an independent spirit and a critical mind. But she could not help Vinnie with the predominant problem of her life. Vinnie was still unfocused in her affections, without direction and purpose in the design of her existence.

It was when I was returning home from my aunt's lodgings, that I chanced to see Evan at the railings of the house, speaking with a ragged and dirty young urchin who was, despite that, of acceptable appearance.

There were many of these young boys in the capital, abandoned by their parents, or having run away from home to seek their fortunes. Beggary or thieving seemed to be all that was open to them, apart from humble jobs such as tending horses while the coachman entered a coffeehouse, or running errands, which in this instance, appeared to be the case.

As I approached, I heard the juvenile's voice on the air, quite clearly. "She bids you be at Veralum Gardens, next to the Law Courts, at four o'clock on Wednesday. Not to be late, she said. You know where the Law Courts are?"

I heard directions given, for the youngster was civil and intelligent. I was glad to see that Evan rewarded him well, and on an impulse, as he ran by me, I also pressed a coin into his grimy but willing hand.

I followed Evan into the house. Nothing was said about this conversation; it was no concern of mine, and Evan did not elaborate on the circumstances.

No doubt it is a summons from Candide for an assignation, I thought, as I removed my shawl upstairs. I glanced out into the Square, but it was empty. This will undoubtedly cheer Evan up, I thought to myself. I was glad that he had arranged an outing with his new acquaintance, though personally I thought the environs of the Law Courts a strange place for a young lady and her beau to meet.

There was more news of preparations for the battle at sea. Lord Nelson had begun to maneuver his ships, placing himself to the windward side of Villeneuve, so that he could cut off the Frenchman's escape.

At dawn on the 21st of October, the enemy's ships were seen silhouetted on the horizon. As soon as Villeneuve spotted Nelson's ships, he ordered his own ships into line of battle, and reversing their course, ordered them to steer north.

All day the two fleets sought to take up the positions from which they would fight. Gun faced gun, and sail faced sail, at a distance. The French fleet could hear the British bands on the poops of the ships playing 'Rule Britannia' and 'Hearts of Oak'.

When the British gun decks were cleared for action the sailors, stripped to the waist, danced hornpipes, and shouted at their adversaries. There was a heavy swell that day. Lord Nelson was below, making some final dispositions, and attending to the paper work which always accompanies battles or great events.

The weaponry officers stood on duty, day and night, without respite. The decks were sanded; the guns gleamed. The whole fleet was ready, awaiting the one circumstance which would give them action and maneuver. The whole of the British fleet awaited the signal flags from the *Victory*'s halyards, and the entire country awaited Lord Nelson's message to his fleet.

That night I could not sleep. The excitement which had seized the country in its grip held me too; I pictured the fleet, the *Victory* as I had seen the ship at Portsmouth, and Miles in the front line with the guns.

For I knew that Miles was no officer who stood aloof from action, but a man who would perform superbly what he asked other men to do. Where the guns fired, there he would be, both to give and to receive. For when gun answered gun, the gun turret casualties were the first to be accounted for.

I got up from my bed, and took a glass of water from the carafe on my bedside table. Again I glanced out at the deserted Square. It was while I stood there in my nightdress and wrap, that a startling thought occurred to me. It had nothing to do with the battle. Nothing to do with Miles or my love, or his danger. I remembered again the young boy speaking to Evan. And heard again the instructions given.

What was I doing to assume that this message came from Candide? I had observed Evan during the evening, and he had certainly shown no elation or pleasure. Had the message then, come from someone else? Had Mrs. Magwich herself instructed Evan to attend at the Veralum Gardens on Wednesday?

At once I was convinced that I had stumbled upon the truth. The clue which I had sought for in London, which I had waited for and hoped for, had been presented to me at last. I would follow Evan to the Veralum Gardens, and see what occurred there.

With the dawn came doubts. Still, I told myself to persist. Even if I were in error, if I saw nothing more than the dainty modiste and Evan chatting together under the shadow of the Law Courts, yet I must observe the assignation; I must follow up the indication, for it was the only clue I had received in London, and it might be my last opportunity to discover the truth.

★ ★ ★

The house in Cavendish Square was now in a ferment of preparations for the departure of Imelda and Robin back to East Quayling. Imelda had purchased a vast amount of fabrics and furnishings to make over Claremont Hall. Robin was indulgent to her. He merely paid the bills.

She had soon recovered from the pain and dislocation of her treatment by Doctor Meredith. I hoped sincerely that the outcome would be successful. Yet, as Doctor Meredith had stressed, Fate itself played a part in these matters.

Aided by Mrs. Bennett, I began to remove my belongings to my aunt's lodgings, for this must be my home when Imelda and Robin had left London. I could not help but feel regret that my beloved friends and I must soon be parted.

There was no further news of the battle at sea, and I had to still my anxieties regarding Miles and his safety. On the morning of Wednesday, I planned my day around the coming appointment in Veralum Gardens. Long before the appointed time, I slipped unnoticed and alone from the house, and approached the Law Courts. Taking up my place in an alleyway which ajoined some legal chambers, I drew back into the shadows and awaited events.

The Veralum Gardens formed a little oasis of trees and rather elderly benches, set beside the towering walls of the courts of justice. I could see barristers walking there with their clients. Plaintiffs awaited their calls, and messenger boys were passing a moment between delivery of briefs. A feeling of doubt assailed me.

Surely, Mrs. Magwich would never summon Evan to a meeting here, beneath the very eyes of the legal system? I almost turned to go, chiding myself for my credulity, when suddenly, I saw the two people whose images were forever etched upon my mind, approaching the gardens quite openly. As if without a care in the world, Mrs.

Magwich and Robert Lessing turned aside, and entered the gardens.

Mrs. Magwich was elaborately dressed in gray silk, with a puce bonnet and a black parasol. Robert had toned down his somewhat bizarre man-about-town clothes, and was dressed in sombre gray, as if he were a lawyer, or at least a client seeking legal assistance.

And as I watched them, my very blood seemed to seethe within me. I marveled at their effrontery, to stroll in the Veralum Gardens, as if they were benefactors to the world, and not the reverse! Yet how like Mrs. Magwich it was, I thought! She had a twisted sense of humour, and no doubt it pleased her greatly to meet a victim here, and to extort money from him, by menace, beneath the very eyes of prosecuting lawyers. I felt that I should never understand this strange woman, not that I truly had any urge to do so. All I wanted was to bring her to justice, to close down her establishment, and to release the prisoners she kept incarcerated there.

Surely enough, Evan arrived. I saw the three talking together. Yet the transaction was not straightforward. Perhaps he was asking them how they knew that he had received some money from his uncle? Perhaps his time in London had stiffened his resolution. Nevertheless, a conversation was taking place, although no money had passed between them as yet. It was now, at this moment, that I had to decide what to do next.

I must certainly follow Mrs. Magwich and Robert to their destination, when the interview with Evan was over. If only I had an ally, I thought. If only . . . It was then that I raised my eyes and saw that the alley adjoined a small lane — Poutney Lane. I remembered that Judge Stanley had his chambers there.

At once I sped down the alley and into the lane. Almost immediately, I saw the brass plate bearing the Judge's name at the entrance to his chambers.

And then, as luck would have it, the Judge himself emerged from the hallway. I called to him, and hastened to his side. In my excitement I held his arm, and detained him while I told him the course of events.

He grasped the situation immediately, and together we hastened to the head of the alleyway, which gave a view of the Veralum Gardens. We were just in time to see Evan hand over a packet to the unsavoury couple, and then the two of them turning aside, to leave the gardens.

"We must follow them," I gasped to the Judge. "Let us take up our places behind them, and trace them back to where they live!"

"Celeste," answered the Judge. "I will do this. But you cannot accompany me. The reason is obvious. If this pair should suspect they are being followed, and turn around, they would recognize you, and be alerted. But as for myself . . . they do not know me. I must do this on my own. Hasten home, my dear. I will follow this pair, and then report the result back to you. Go quickly. They are moving away."

The judge left me, and emerged from the alleyway. His movements were calm, almost casual, as if he were a legal gentleman enjoying the air, which he was. He took up his position several paces behind Mrs. Magwich and Robert Lessing. I saw the evil pair, smiling, then laughing. Robert Lessing was holding Mrs. Magwich's arm. But the Judge kept his even pace behind them; he did not falter or move aside. And so the strange trio left the environs of the Law Courts, and were lost to view.

★ ★ ★

At the time we did not know it. We were informed of it later — that just before the battle Lord Nelson had gone below to his own quarters, and put his affairs in order.

He made his will and wrote in his

diary. His prayer was for victory, for his country, for his soul, and for the humane future of the British navy. He then composed his immortal words to his fighting men, calling upon all to perform to the limit of their endurance and their lives.

Following this, Lord Nelson signaled for close action, and then called for anchor before dark, since a gale was rising from the west and the shallows of Trafalgar lay ahead like traps for his ships. And so the decisions were made. The battle of Trafalgar was begun, a battle that was to have an important bearing upon our country's future. And drastic results upon my own personal life.

# 12

IT was not until the next day that Judge Stanley visited the house in Cavendish Square, to inform me of the results of his actions.

I had waited in a fever of impatience, tormented by fantasies of various kinds, even imagining the noble Judge set upon, assaulted and killed. He arrived in the evening, and was accompanied by an official of the Bow Street runners.

The whole family assembled to hear the news, for I had informed them of the Judge's pursuit of Mrs. Magwich and Robert Lessing. They were as anxious as I was to hear the outcome of the measured chase.

"I followed the two persons in question," the Judge told me, "to a house in Isleworth where they lived and had their establishment. It was in an outwardly respectable street in

270

a good neighbourhood, though many neighbours realized that something was wrong. None, however, had the courage to inform the police.

"When I had ascertained the exact address, I returned to the Law Courts, and saw the Sheriff of the City of London whom, I am glad to say, I number among my friends. Without delay, he ordered an official raid on the premises. The whole operation was uncovered, and Mrs. Flora Magwich and Robert Lessing were arrested. They are in the cells of Newington Gaol, and charges are being prepared."

He turned to me. "We must thank you, Miss Celeste, for your vigilance and determination. Without you, these two people would still be free."

The official then asked me for my testimony, and also inquired whether I would testify at the trial. I agreed to do this, and the Judge and the police officer left us without much more ado.

I had watched Evan during this

interview. He had been silent, although blood had seemed to drain from his face. When we were alone at a turning on the stairs, I said, "You are free now, Evan, free of these people who have taken your money and ruined your life."

"Yes, I am free now," he said thoughtfully. He attempted to express his gratitude, but I did not wish this. I saw the tears stand in his eyes. "What are your plans for the future, Evan?" I asked him on an impulse.

"I do not know," he said after a pause. "The respite I was forced to enjoy here, in London, from my former social engagements, has caused my earlier cravings to wane somewhat.

"I have seen much of my uncle lately. I enjoyed our visit to the museum, and now he has asked me to accompany him to a group of almshouses, that he is considering endowing. I find I have quite a flair for this sort of thing, Celeste," he added awkwardly, and laughed.

It was lovely to see his face light up again. We did not know that the matter was still not over for Evan. But for now, we both felt happiness at the outcome. The future would unfold itself in time.

★ ★ ★

The British fleet sailed in two divisions as planned: one led by Admiral Collingwood, and the other by Lord Nelson. As soon as the front line ships came within the range of enemy fire they were forced to withstand a terrible concentration of cannonading and shot. Sails were torn away and timbers shattered. Still, the ships sailed on, seeking the breakthrough in the enemy lines.

The *Victory* was steered close to the *Bucenture*, which was Villeneuve's flagship. The *Victory* raked her with a sixty-eight pounder, and shattered her decks with a double-shotted broadside. But the *Victory* was herself assailed by

273

the *Neptune* and the *Redoubtable*. The ships were locked together, riggings almost touching and guns facing guns, muzzle to muzzle.

The battle raged around the *Victory*. But the crew of the *Redoubtable* specialized in close arm fighting, grenade throwing, boarding and sniping from the upper reaches. These snipers assailed the *Victory*'s upper decks, fifty feet below them. Their close and devastating fire was difficult to withstand.

Lord Nelson and Admiral Hardy paced together on the quarterdeck, directing the whole operation. To Admiral Hardy's surprise, Lord Nelson has insisted on wearing a dress coat on which were silhouetted his four stars of chivalry. He carried no sword. For the first time in his life in battle, he had left his sword in his cabin. It was as if he had deliberately made himself a target for enemy fire.

A musket shot from a French sniper high in the rigging penetrated

Lord Nelson's shoulder and chest and entered his spine. He fell to the deck, as if he had slipped in the inevitable blood of warfare, his hand touching the deck. Then he fell to his side.

He was helped below. His personal physician, Beatty, attended him. Internal bleeding weakened his resistance. His staff did everything possible, but Nelson knew that his time was short.

He lay in his cabin and listened to the noise of battle; he heard cheers from the gun decks above as the heavy shots reached their mark. The *Victory* shook in the returning fire. The climax of the battle was reached, and then the fury began to wane. News was brought below to Nelson's bedside.

The victory had been won, and fifteen of the French ships had surrendered. "I had bargained for twenty," Nelson said. He instructed Hardy where to anchor, and spoke of Lady Hamilton, and his provisions for her. "Remember," he said, "I leave Lady Hamilton and my daughter Horatia as a legacy to my country." He slipped into unconsciousness, and at four-thirty on the 21st of October, 1805, almost three hours after he had been hit, Lord Nelson died.

Not one British ship had been lost in this battle, yet two-thirds of the enemy fleet was immobilized. The dreadful threat of invasion by Napoleon which had threatened England was finally removed. We could dwell in peace and security for some time.

The country went wild with joy at the victory, but the rejoicing was overshadowed by Lord Nelson's death. A voluntary period of mourning hushed the nation. And those with men who had fought in this battle awaited news of casualties, and news of those who had survived and would return.

★ ★ ★

I knew that something was wrong as soon as Robin entered the house in Cavendish Square. He and Imelda were

276

dressed and in readiness to travel to East Quayling. Indeed, their trunks had already gone ahead, and they had arranged for their carriage within an hour.

"I have just seen Judge Stanley," Robin said. "He has received grievous news from the admiralty, Celeste, prepare yourself. Miles has been killed in the battle of Trafalgar.

"A broadside from the *Redoubtable* demolished the guns of which Miles was in charge. There were no survivors. The emplacements were shattered, and there was no possibility of withstanding the bombardment.

"Judge Stanley asked me to relay these tidings to you. He seemed concerned for you. He seemed concerned for you. He . . . " But Robin's voice broke, and he could not continue. The tears streamed down Imelda's face at the loss of her old and valued friend. Neither could continue and they took me into their arms.

My two friends offered to postpone

their return to East Quayling, but I refused to allow them to delay their journey. Accompanied by Mrs. Bennett, I returned to my aunt's lodgings, and told her the news. Both she and Miss Preston were quite distressed on my behalf.

I felt that I wanted to be alone. I went out, unaccompanied, and walked across Cavendish Square into the city of London, walking the streets until I was exhausted from the exertion. It was as if I wished to drown my emotional pain in physical effort; but the physical effort brought me no assuagement of my grief.

I had heard it said that for a fiancée to lose her lover brought less sorrow than for a wife to lose a husband. This must be true. It is logical; it is natural, but it was not true in my case.

And I was not even a fiancée. I had been rejected by the man I so dearly loved! And yet this made no difference. It was to me as if my heart and my life had been lost with the guncasings of the *Victory*. Miles had passed on to another world and had taken my life with him. The woman who now tramped London's streets was an empty shell.

I had by this time reached Blackfriar's Bridge. To my amazement, I saw that the Bridge was crowded with people, and that a great concourse lined the banks of the Thames.

"What is the cause of this occasion, if you please?" I asked a respectable looking woman nearby. She looked at me with surprise.

"'Tis Lord Nelson," she said. "Have you not heard? Do you not know what is happening?

"They are bringing Lord Nelson's body from his ship the *Victory* at Trafalgar, up the Thames to the admiralty.

"See, the barge and its naval escort have left Greenwich, and are approaching this bridge."

My unknown friend burst into tears, and clung to the parapet of the bridge.

All around her were likewise affected. I gazed upstream and saw the naval flotilla approaching.

It seemed that hundred of boats, with sailors at their oars, were accompanying the one vessel which flew Lord Nelson's flag. Many naval officers lined this burial vessel; the whole fleet seemed to be present, at attention, yet in respectful postures.

The waters of the Thames could hardly be seen for the motion of oars, the coloured uniforms of the sailors, the flags of fighting ships, the oak hulks of the boats. It seemed, as this flotilla approached Blackfriars Bridge, that history itself was incarnate before us. For many, the occasion was too much, and women fainted, while men wept openly. A great cry, both of honour and suffering, was heard, as the burial barge and the flotilla passed under the bridge.

I returned home to my Aunt's lodgings. She was concerned for me, and had been at the window watching out for me. As I entered, she clasped me in her arms, and Miss Preston went to make us all an infusion of herbal tea.

We sat together on the sofa in the window overlooking the place. My Aunt spoke to me with a show of determination and common sense.

"I understand your grief, my dear, but after all, you were not affianced to this young man, and there was no formal understanding between you. Indeed, the reverse was the case. Therefore, I pray you look to the future, and put his unhappy phase behind you. You have still your life to live, and your future to create along purposeful lines."

When I did not answer, she continued. "Your stay in England has not all been plain sailing. Indeed, to my mind, you have suffered greatly, and the time and the occasions of these disasters must cease. I have myself been to the Belgian Embassy. I did not see Ralph, of course, but an official informed me that now that the battle of Trafalgar has been fought and won, the seas are to be immediately opened, and commercial and other traffic will soon be resumed. Indeed, he told me that next week the packet will be sailing from London to Antwerp, or even Bruges. Therefore . . . Look to the future, Celestine. We will return home, and start afresh."

I bowed my head as Miss Preston entered with the tea. I tried to drink the brew, and it refreshed me. Admist the loving glances of the two ladies who were my true family, I assented. I accepted all that had been said. I would quit England forthwith, and return to my home in Bruges.

# 13

I TRIED now to put on as bold a face as I could upon circumstances, and busied myself with preparations for our return to Belgium.

Yet nothing could stem the secret emotions of my heart. I mentioned them to no one. I bore my feelings alone.

In a strange way, I longed to see Judge Stanley. Beyond our last meeting, he had not been in touch. I longed to help ease his pain at Miles' death, though how I could do this, I did not know.

I thought the Judge had many of the stalwart characteristics of my own father, an inner dependability, a farsightedness, a generosity of spirit that was still realistic and firm. Yet I had no status in his life, beyond that of a discarded friend of his son. It was not likely that he would approach me in any way.

I was greatly surprised at this time, to find that I had a new friend, or rather an old acquaintance who appeared to have changed her attitude. Vinnie called frequently at our lodgings, and brought always a small posy of flowers, a confection, or small gift.

There was a new air about her; she appeared more tentative in her approach to things, and not so dogmatic and imperious. She was remaining in London, she said. I wondered who had wrought this change in her, but she said nothing, and I did not ask.

Within a few days Evan called to see me. He appeared upset and ill at ease. I wondered if he was in some trouble with Candide, but when he spoke to me it was upon a different matter.

"I have had a visit from the police," he told me. "My name and address were found in the records of the bordello, and the magistrate has asked me to attend for an interview.

"In addition, in order to pay Mrs. Magwich and Robert Lessing, I have become hopelessly in debt here in London. I borrowed money from userers, and they are pressing me for payment. I have no hope of clearing the amount, and ruin on these two counts stares me in the face."

I went to the sideboard and poured a cup of coffee for Evan from a pot which was still warm, and he appeared refreshed by his first sip. Then, in his agitation, he knocked the cup and its contents to the floor, and we both watched the dregs of the coffee seep into the carpet.

It was at this moment, that a strange incident occurred. It seemed as though the stain on the carpet had formed itself into a shape. The vague shape of a horse and coach. And in that moment it was as if a final clearing wind blew through my mind, and the last missing vestige of my memory returned.

"Evan," I said, "when you came out of Mrs. Magwich's premises, what did you do? Was the carriage still waiting for you?"

Evan stared at me in perplexity. "Why, yes, to my surprise it was. I addressed the coachman in angry terms, for his playing such a stupid hoax on me. He laughed, and . . . "

"You raised your stick," I said. "You did not threaten the coachman, but you waved it to reinforce your words!"

"Yes, that is so, Celeste. How did you know?"

"You then took off your cloak before entering the carriage, and the coachman drove you away," I continued abstractedly. I faced Evan directly.

"Don't you see, Evan, I saw you? I saw you as I ran down the street from the bordello. I saw the carriage, and you getting into it, and the stick and your cloak, and . . . you. My memory has totally returned, Evan. I saw you leaving the bordello. There is no doubt about that!"

It took Evan a moment or two to assimilate the information. Then a light seemed to dawn in his eyes. "Celeste, you see what this means, don't you. And you see clearly my future course? I must go at once to the authorities and then to my uncle, for your testimony clears me forever of the official accusation and the doubts of everyone concerned. I have sought the coachman everywhere but have not been able to find him. But your testimony supports my own evidence, without need of the coachman's confirmation."

"But what about your debts?" I asked.

"Never mind about the debts! If my uncle is displeased I can emigrate. Better men than I have had to take this course. I beg you to accompany me, Celeste. Could we not start again? We liked one another when we first met."

"But what of Candide?" I asked him.

He expressed surprise. "She has married her benefactor, a man older and far richer than myself. I am heart free, Celeste. For Vinnie also has found another attachment, and her heart is firmly fixed elsewhere."

I did not make any enquiries into this new circumstance, and indeed to me, the whole affair seemed to be getting out of hand. "I am sorry, Evan," I said. "I value your friendship, and will always do so. But for me, the prospect of any deeper liaison is now over. That is all behind me now, for good."

I knew that I would never look at another man with deep emotion, even with Miles gone. My love for him would not die, but would endure so long as I lived. Evan said no more, but soon went away.

★ ★ ★

The occasion of Lord Nelson's funeral was a day of national mourning, for the British people felt they had lost more than a revered naval commander. They had lost an ideal, a pattern, the personification of a new and revolutionary way of life.

His personal concern for the naval personnel under his command had set a new standard of care and comfort for the Navy. Admiral Nelson's example stamped a new and more humane influence on life at sea, which was to endure through many decades, and which would be copied throughout the world.

On the day of his burial, all shops were closed; no one worked, and the capital and the nation halted.

The funeral procession began from the admiralty, and progressed to St. Paul's Cathedral. Black horses with plumes and draperies drew the ornate ebony funeral hearse. The air was hushed; there was only the sound of the horses, the marching mourners, and the sobs of those in the crowd who were too overcome to endure in silence.

So great was the concourse of mourners that the ranks stretched from the admiralty to St. Paul's without a break. The service had already begun in the Cathedral, before the followers at the end of the concourse began their march.

My aunt and Miss Preston and I went on foot to see the funeral, as near to St. Paul's as we could get. There were many women in widow's weeds around us; I knew that the casualties had been high at Trafalgar; the victory had not been gained with ease, and without loss of valued men.

A great sigh went up from the concourse, as the hearse approached. We watched the burial party enter the cathedral, and then we went away.

We spoke little. There seemed nothing to say. Universal mourning spoke for us all, and private grief had already been expressed. There was only the future now, bleak and uncompromising though this appeared. It seemed that with the burial of Lord Nelson the future beckoned us forward implacably. And I knew that I and my small family must move forward to keep pace.

When we reached our lodgings, it was to find a message from the Belgian Embassy stating that the packet would be sailing for Bruges two days from now, and that our passages had been booked on it.

So Fate itself seemed to be moving me swiftly from all that had happened in England. We began to pack for our final return to Bruges.

Yet in some incredible way, the scene of Lord Nelson's funeral drew me still. I felt I must go by myself, unaccompanied, to St. Paul's Cathedral, to pay my final respects to the man who had been so kind to Miles, and who had overshadowed our lives.

★ ★ ★

It was three days after the burial. Lord Nelson's body was resting in the marble sarcophagus which had been prepared for Cardinal Wolsey.

Many other citizens were making their solitary pilgrimages. The funeral flowers were wilting a little now; people walked sedately, or in pairs, observing the funeral decorations. There was no one that I knew. Then suddenly, I was arrested in my progress by the sight of a figure that I recognized.

The lady before me was of stoutish build, with a rounded, and rather unconfined figure. She wore a dress of brown silk with floating panels, which added to her bulk, and a large hat with a long veil. She carried a furled parasol, which she leaned on as she walked. Behind her moved the maid I had seen at Merton. Lady Hamilton was attended, yet alone.

Through the veil I could see the beauty of her features, the nobility of her brow, and the azure gleam of her eyes. Many men had fallen in love with Lady Hamilton; many had sought her favours. They would not do so now. Yet still, beneath the veil, the remnants of her beauty and enchantment remained.

I stood still. I was at a loss as to

what to do, whether to acknowledge Lady Hamilton, or to respect her clear desire for privacy. It was obvious that no one else in the crypt realized her identity.

My wonderings were halted when she herself noticed me, and I saw the light of recognition in her eyes. She came to my side, moving easily, though slowly, and halted before me.

"Celeste," she said. "For I may call you that, surely? You are here, too, to pay your private respects to Lord Nelson. He liked you, my dear. He gave you a rose from the garden at Merton, did he not? The Trafalgar rose, he called it. Do you remember? It was like a flash of prophecy, that. As if he knew where the final battle would be fought, and what would be his fate."

"I trust I may offer you my sincere condolences, Lady Hamilton," I said.

She thanked me, absently. Her expression was abstracted. "You will know that Lord Nelson left myself, and Horatia, as a legacy to the nation. This was a clear indication that he expected a grateful government and king to provide for us in a liberal, or at least an adequate way.

"But now, they have honoured his brother with an earldom, and a pension of £5,000 a year. And Fanny, his wife, has been voted a pension for life of £2,000. But for myself, there is nothing."

I was shocked at this news — and saddened.

"There is also a rumour that the earl will be granted a huge sum of money to purchase an estate," Lady Hamilton continued. "And Lord Nelson's sisters will be voted £15,000 each. So much generosity! So much magnanimity to honour Lord Nelson's memory and his name! But for the one who worshipped him and cared for him through difficult times . . . his government has granted less than nothing. And I feel the rebuff keenly. Not least that Lord Nelson's last wish, as he lay dying, should have been disregarded and set at naught."

I did not know what to say to Lady Hamilton. Perhaps silence was the best reply. I did not know then, though it was soon to be commonly known, that Lord Nelson had left what he had to Lady Hamilton, but it was too little to be significant. The future outlook for her was bleak indeed.

Neither of us could foresee the long slide which was now to begin for Emma Hamilton. The slide into poverty, self-indulgence and misfortune. The debtors' prison, the exile in France. And her death, fifteen years later, in Calais.

For the moment we simply stood facing one another, near to the sarcophagus, a little apart from the crowds. I saw tears stand in her brilliant eyes.

"I have been to the Greenwich Naval Hospital this morning," she continued finally. "To see the survivors of the *Victory*. Lord Nelson would have wished me to do this, and believe me, I was received by his men with gratitude and honour."

"I am sure of their appreciation," I said. "Were many men saved from the battering the ship received?"

"Not many," she said. "But I knew several by name. One man particularly, it pleased me to see. A neighbour of ours at East Quayling — Miles Stanley. He had been blown into the water by the force of the explosion, when . . . "

"Miles Stanley?" I cried, and I heard my voice on the air, unnaturally loud. "Did you say that Miles is alive, and in the Naval Hospital at Greenwich?"

"That is so," she said. "Did you not know this? You were friends were you not? Now I recall — it was rumoured at Merton that you would make a match of it!"

I explained quickly the misunderstanding between Miles and myself.

"Go to him, Celeste," Lady Hamilton responded. "Do not let anything stand in your way. If you care for Miles

Stanley, go to him, and go at once. Love is the most important thing in life," she told me earnestly. "I myself am witness to this. And whatever may happen to me in the future will be a price I will willingly pay for the love I have known. Therefore . . . "

"May I ask you to please excuse me, Lady Hamilton?" I said. I did not wish for the celebrated lady to lecture me on the importance of love, for I knew of love's importance. I had felt its impact and its influence in my own life.

Her news was the important matter to me. Miles alive! "I think he has not long to live," she was adding somberly. "But you can at least ease his passing . . . "

I curtsied to her, and turned to speed away. I sensed that she stood watching me for a long time.

Outside St. Paul's I saw an empty carriage, and asked the coachman if he would take me to the hospital at Greenwich.

"But this is a private carriage, miss,"

he protested. Then a light came into his eyes. "But my master has been a naval man like myself, and would wish me to assist those whose relatives have been wounded in battle."

So saying, he opened the carriage door, shook the reins, and his horse moved briskly towards Greenwich.

At the hospital there was chaos. Casualties had been brought in from whom there was no room. Medicines were scarce. The staff had run out of swabs and bandages.

Doctors were rushed off their feet, and the rough and ready nurses, many of large build and forthright manner, coped as best they could.

Relatives thronged the corridors and wards. Many had brought rum and soup; some carried food in baskets, spare clothing and bedding. Small wonder that the wounded lay exhausted upon the floor or their makeshift beds. The aroma of human suffering and discharge was all pervasive.

I found Miles at last. I was directed

to the ward in which he lay. But on the threshold of the room I halted.

What I was going to do was unorthodox, even unseemly for the times. I was going to see a man who had rejected me . . . to tell him of my love and my deep and long-lasting caring.

It was not important to me that I was defying convention; that I was brushing aside the accepted code of this year 1805. It was not important to me that I might — indeed, almost certainly should — receive a further rejection. The only thing that mattered was to see Miles again, to offer him what comfort I could. And if, as Lady Hamilton had said, I should see him for the last time, then I wished that he should know of my devotion — and I wished to have the imprint of his face in my memory for the rest of my life.

There had been a hawker at the doors of the hospital selling small sugar cakes and sweetmeats, and with an offering of these, I approached Miles' bed. The sight of him cut me to the heart.

He was deathly pale and emaciated. I could see no sign of physical injuries, but clearly the violent shock of the explosion had affected him, and his long immersion in the water had almost taken his life.

He opened his eyes at my approach, and I saw a gleam of recognition in his eyes. "Celeste," he said, and put out a trembling hand towards me. I sank beside the palliasse, on which he was laid, and took his hand in mine. It seemed that we were both too overcome to speak.

I indicated the cakes, but he shook his head. "I am unable to eat or drink," he said. "Yet without food the doctors assure me I shall die. If this is to be the case," he said. "I must tell you first . . . "

Miles struggled to sit up a little on his rough mattress and addressed me earnestly. "Ralph van de Meuve came to see me," he said. "He was obliged to visit the *Victory* on the day before we sailed for battle, with a personal message for Lord Nelson from the Belgian King. And when his official business was done, Ralph sought me out in the wardroom. And there he told me ... he told me the true circumstances of your feelings, Celeste. That you did not love him, and had already ended your engagement."

I listened with tears slipping down my cheeks.

"Ralph told me also of your admission of love for myself. Love which, he assured me, was firm and constant. He commended me to seek you out at the end of the battle, and to declare myself to you."

Here Miles paused to gather strength. "For yes, Celeste, I loved you then, and I love you now. My love has never faltered. Even during battle your face was always before me, your name on my lips. Can you ever forgive me for my harsh words to you? I see now that they were without foundation, and do me no credit."

I could not help the overflowing of my emotion. "There is nothing to forgive," I said. "Your reaction was a natural one, I see that clearly. But we have now only to save your life, and get you well. And God knows, I can see that this is a formidable task."

At this moment we were interrupted by the arrival of Judge Stanley, who had also just heard the news of Miles' delivery from death. I watched the meeting of father and son, and begged to withdraw from their reunion. But both men asked me to stay. The three of us seemed united in an inescapable bond, as we sat at Miles' bedside.

The Judge went off to see Miles' doctor and soon returned. "There are no physical injuries, only the effects of bombardment and drowning. Many men are so affected, and the doctors deem their injuries as serious as broken bones."

The Judge and I were combined

in a resolve to restore Miles' health. "He must return to our home at East Quayling. Celeste, could you not come back to Riverside House, now that Imelda is in residence there, and aid my household in caring for Miles? I feel that your presence will be worth more to him than any medicines and therapies." And the Judge smiled at me with understanding, in that moment welcoming me into his life.

I returned in the Judge's carriage to my aunt's lodgings, and told her and Miss Preston what had occurred. They agreed to put off their return to Bruges for a week, and my aunt gave her instant consent for me to return to East Quayling.

★ ★ ★

Imelda sent a letter that my room at Riverside House was prepared. But before I left London, I had one more duty to perform. Evan and I had already visited the police, and Evan had been in touch with his uncle. Lord Stanhope, therefore, sent a message round by a servant requesting the presence of Evan and myself at the evening dinner.

Both Evan and I dressed with care, knowing that this was an important occasion. Lord Stanhope received us kindly, and indeed, was affectionate and welcoming in his attitude.

I was impressed, even overawed by Lord Stanhope's house in the new district of Knightsbridge. It was spacious, beautifully kept, and filled with paintings and antiquities. Yet it was no museum, but a well-loved home.

An appetizing meal was served, and both Evan and I found that we were hungry, and enjoyed the repast. Afterwards, in the drawing room, without any more ado, Evan began to tell his uncle of the sequence of events concerning the bordello, and I reinforced his testimony where necessary. Lord Stanhope heard us out with fairness and consideration.

Evan told his uncle also of the months of extortion which had followed, and Lord Stanhope understood this too, and the reasons behind Evan's wish to keep the matter from him. "But now that I have obtained my release, thanks to the efforts of Celeste and Judge Stanley," Evan said, "I wish you to know the truth. I will accept your censure, for I realize that my past life could not have met with your approval at any time."

Lord Stanhope sipped his wine reflectively. I saw his shrewd gray eyes fixed upon Evan. Then a smile touched his lips.

"But of course I was aware of your mode of life, Evan, and had kept track of your activities for some time.

"In the clubs of London your gambling escapades were often discussed. It is difficult to live a secret life when the whole of society observes your actions.

"I do not censure you unduly," Lord Stanhope said. "It is an inevitable thing for a young man to kick over the traces. It is better to have one's moments of rebellion early, rather than later.

"To be profligate late in life makes a man a sorry spectacle. I do not think that this will happen to you," he added. "I will clear your debts and discharge the userers. This period of your life is over, and we must now begin a more creative and constructive course."

Evan was almost too overcome to stammer his thanks. Lord Stanhope did not amplify his statements at this moment, but went on to speak of the closing of the bordello. This also had been discussed in London society, and many young men, some of noble birth, had been released from bondage when the bawdy house was closed.

The evening progressed in a pleasant way. I could see that Evan was overcome with joy at his uncle's actions, and lack of reproach. It was clear that he cared deeply for Lord Stanhope, who stood to him in the relationship of a father. He had been desolate to think of losing his uncle's approval. Now that this had been granted, he was relieved, and filled with gratitude.

In the hallway, at the end of the evening, when we were about to depart, Lord Stanhope said, "A small present for Celeste to thank her for her efforts, the results of which have meant much to me, I assure you."

He then presented me with a small, exquisitely coloured enamel box. And to Evan he added, "I plan to leave England for Spain, to see the Escorial, and to see also a scheme of education they are establishing there. If you would care to accompany me to Spain, Evan, we will see Philip the Second's memorial, and also make some judgement upon this school.

"I valued your opinions before; you showed both wit and discernment. And during this excursion into Europe, we will discuss your future, and come to some conclusions about your career."

I returned to Riverside House, and

then spent much time at the Judge's House. The struggle to restore Miles to health was a hard one. His system had imbibed so much poison from the waters of Trafalgar, that it seemed as though his frame would never be normal. Yet, bit by bit, we persevered, until finally he could take sips of plain water and small fragments of food. We won our battle, as Miles had won his. For it was his gun which had raked the *Redoubtable*, and which had played its part in bringing the French fleet to surrender. He was commended in a dispatch from the admiralty, and promoted to captain upon his recall.

Imelda married Robin in a brilliant and beautiful ceremony which the whole county attended. But Miles and I were married in a simple ceremony in Bruges, for as soon as Miles was well enough to travel, I returned to my home, to be with my family. This was my duty and I felt I owed it to my aunt and Miss Preston, who had done so much for me.

To my surprise, just before the marriage, my aunt — prompted by Miss Preston — invited Vinnie to visit us. Vinnie begged that she might attend me at the ceremony, and this was arranged.

Ralph was a guest at our wedding, of course, and again to my surprise, I found that he paid some attention to Vinnie at the reception. I heard them arranging a date for Ralph to escort her to the more picturesque quarter of Bruges.

Ralph and Vinnie were married almost a year after our own ceremony. In Ralph's directness, his authority, her certainty, Vinnie found what she had unconsciously been seeking. He curbed her moods. She mellowed, and became more tolerant and kindly in her attitude. She accepted the restraints he placed upon her and he himself had found a woman who could respond to his dominant nature.

Madame van de Meuve was at first taken aback when Ralph told her that he wished to marry an Englishwoman, but Vinnie's money, which was regarded as a dowry, did much to placate her. Vinnie loved La Jola — the square house with the square furniture. And she went on to become one of the most prominent ladies of Bruges, entertaining and being entertained in fine style.

What can I say of my own marriage? The unity of Miles and myself? It had a felicity that never wavered, and a unison of aims that was never in question.

Upon her marriage to Robin, Imelda went to live at Claremont Hall. Thus Riverside House became vacant, for upon their return from Spain, Lord Stanhope invited Evan to make his permanent home with him in Knightsbridge, and to join him in his activities and his life.

They were reformers and, yes, there was much to reform at this time. But they had a liveliness, a sense of enjoyment, a grace in living that removed any puritanism from their ventures. Evan did not marry, and in time, upon his uncle's decease, he inherited not only his fortune, but his title. Sometimes I think he regretted the loss of Candide, but I did not know for certain if this was so.

Miles and I went to live at Riverside House. This was at the express invitation of Imelda and Robin. A peppercorn rent, they said. They really wished to keep the place warm and occupied. And so the house which had given me solace and refuge when I was battered and bruised, without a memory or identity, became my home, and the home of my family. Aunt Adelaide and Miss Preston visited us, and the house rang with laughter and gaiety.

After ten months of her marriage, Imelda bore her first child, a daughter, to the great delight of us all. Lady Hamilton remained our friend, until she left Merton. The house became run-down. Sometimes I thought I could see the small, slim, indomitable figure of Lord Nelson, walking in the garden. But he had gone too. Although his legacy to the navy and his country was to remain forever.

When Miles had recovered, he was recalled to the service. He was given his own ship, and sent on an expedition to the West Indies. I remained at home awaiting the arrival of our first child, who was to be born within the sound of the River Wandle, in the old house beneath the open Surrey skies. And close to the village of East Quayling, which had granted me refuge, and which was to become, for the rest of my life, my well-beloved and honoured home.

## THE END